Ex Libris

"Lance has looked after me for years."

Marisa offered the explanation as they drove away.

"Has he?" Dirk sounded skeptical. "He could have been stricter a few years ago."

Marisa flushed and stared out at the countryside. "He had to be away a lot," she said stiffly. "But he looked after my schooling and, well, everything. My affairs—"

"Your affairs?"

"My money. . . my business affairs," she said, irritated, and added explosively, "You have a low opinion of me, haven't you? All because of that . . . that night. That's why you kissed me the way you did yesterday, isn't it?"

He turned to give her a cool glance. "No, it isn't. The simple fact is, you're not fifteen now," he said laconically. "So you can expect to be kissed that way."

Harlequin Premiere Editions

Harlequin
Premiere
Editions

THE
KURRANULLA
ROUND

Dorothy Cork

Harlequin Books

TORONTO • LONDON • LOS ANGELES • AMSTERDAM
SYDNEY • HAMBURG • PARIS • STOCKHOLM • ATHENS • TOKYO

Original hardcover edition published in 1979
by Mills & Boon Limited

ISBN 0-373-82106-9

This Harlequin Premiere Editions volume
published October 1981

THE KURRANULLA ROUND

CHAPTER ONE

IT was so hot in the hotel bedroom that Matty Segal was tempted to put on a sleeveless white cotton dress and sandals. But who was going to look at her in that, out at the Kurranulla race course? Her uncle Jerry, who was a bookmaker, might protest that all he wanted was for her to enjoy herself, meet people—meaning men, of course—but Matty had other ideas.

'A glamorous woman can be an asset to a bookmaker —a draw-card,' Maisie had said once, when Matty was watching her pack ready to go away with Jerry to the provincial races. 'Well, I'm not glamorous now and never was, but at least I can be eye-catching. You know —wear real bright colours, something gypsyish and out of the ordinary like this outfit—lots of make-up, a big come-on smile for the men—all that kind of thing.'

Maisie had obviously loved the race meetings and it was a pity she couldn't have gone away with Jerry more often. Matty wasn't certain whether it was because of her that she had mostly stayed home in Perth, or whether it was because her sister Louise depended on her help at Peppertree Lodge, where Matty lived too. It was a private hotel in a riverside suburb of Perth, and it belonged to Maisie's widowed sister, Louise Wright, and Matty had only discovered this year, after her aunt died and she herself was the one to work for Louise, just how much there was to do.

Now, far away in Kurranulla, she stood hesitating, the white dress, appealing in its simplicity, held against her slender body, her grey-green eyes looking back at her perplexedly from the mirror. With her nut-brown hair and lightly freckled nose, she looked possibly less than her almost twenty years, and in a straight white dress she'd be no draw-card, that much was certain. With a sigh of regret, she hung the dress in the wardrobe and fished out from her suitcase the gear she had bought in Perth especially for now. That had been a week ago, after Jerry had telephoned down from Port Hedland to make final arrangements about meeting her in Derby, so she could come with him on the Kurranulla round.

She hadn't given much thought to how hot it was going to be in the North-West, and she looked at her clothes ruefully. Gypsy clothes were not for her, and she had chosen tight black jeans, and this flame-coloured shirt—she had an emerald green one as well, with a wide collar and a deeply plunging V-neckline. There were black boots with high heels, a wide gold-studded black leather belt, and, to complete the outfit a hat—a fantastic black ten-gallon hat, with a high crown and a curly brim. Get into that and use eye make-up and lipstick lavishly, and Matty Segal would really look something—even if she didn't look much like Matty Segal!

She began to dress. But she balked at the stiff black jeans; she was going to die of heat in those. She looked in her suitcase again and the first thing she saw was a pair of white shorts. She looked at them longingly, and then, recklessly, she put them on. After all, why not? They were cool, and she wouldn't need the hot leather belt around her waist. And she'd certainly be eye-catching!

She pulled on the boots and stood back to look at herself in the mirror and almost laughed. She grabbed the hat and put it on and made a comical face at herself. Oh heavens! She was going to look more than a little bit outrageous by the time she'd got to work with mascara and eye-shadow. What would Maisie think if she could see her now? In imagination, she heard the rather nasally Australian voice of Jerry's wife telling her cheerfully, 'You look good-oh, Matty. The punters'll be around Jerry's stand like wrens around a cheese board. Don't forget to smile, though!'

Matty tried to smile and discovered unexpectedly that she was nervous. She'd never been to the provincial races before, and it really wasn't her thing to set out to attract men—to be come-onish, as Maisie so lightly put it. In fact, she wouldn't have come up for the round at all if she hadn't been worried about Jerry. The North-West at race time, with country people coming in from hundreds of miles around, was the last place she'd have chosen to visit—for a very private and personal reason that she'd have died rather than confess to Jerry, who was so eager to have her with him for a few weeks. He'd suffered a slight heart attack some weeks previously when he was away from Perth, and he'd been in hospital—though he hadn't admitted to it until later. After that, he'd taken ten days rest at Peppertree Lodge, and it was during that time he'd suggested Matty should accompany him up north.

'There's no future for you here, running your legs off all day helping Louise keep this show going—sitting over the accounts all night,' he'd said. 'You aren't meeting any young people—you've got no marriage prospects.'

'I don't mind,' Matty had protested. 'I don't want to get married, Uncle Jerry—not for years yet. Aunt Louise needs me here just now, and after all, she's given me a home all these years.'

Jerry had frowned. 'It's not good enough. Your mother wouldn't like it. Besides——' He'd stopped and given her a long curiously veiled look, and then he'd grimaced. 'You're too young and pretty to spend your life this way. You've had no fun at all since you left school, not even that trip to Europe we'd planned

for you to take with Maisie before she was taken ill
... How many boy-friends have you had?'

Matty shrugged. The fact was, she'd had no real
boy-friends. She'd been too tied up since she left school
what with her aunt's illness and her work at the hotel.
Not that she cared. She didn't particularly want boy-
friends—and quite positively, she didn't want to run
the risk of meeting up with—certain people she preferred to forget, people who lived in the area Jerry
wanted to take her to.

Somehow she'd managed to put him off by pleading
that it would be unfair to leave Louise stranded, and
promising she would try to find a replacement—a
promise she rather meanly didn't intend to keep. So
Jerry had left Perth alone, though he was going to telephone her from Port Hedland in a couple of weeks'
time.

'You can fly up to Derby, Matty—I'll pick you up
there. Now mind, I'm trusting you to fix things up—
I'm serious about this holiday for you,' he'd said before he left. But Matty had done nothing at all about
looking for someone to take over from her—not until
days later when Louise had aired her views about
Jerry.

'Jerry Bridle's looking his age these days. I wouldn't
mind betting he's been drowning his sorrows in drink
—he's been right up to his neck in money troubles
since Sunshooter had to be destroyed. That I know
for a fact. Well, he shouldn't have bought another
racehorse—he never had any luck with them ... I always predicted he'd go too far and, it was no surprise
to me when he had that heart attack. Gamblers go on
and on until they destroy themselves, and that's what
your uncle is—a gambler. If you ask me, the sooner
you get control of your money the better, Matty. I
sometimes wonder how much'll be left of the pile your
mother left you, by the time you turn twenty-one.'

Matty had worried about her uncle after that. Was he drinking? Did he really have money troubles? It had never occurred to her before that he might; he'd always seemed to have plenty to spare for anything Maisie had wanted. Of course, it had been a terrible blow to him when Sunshooter had broken his leg only weeks after he'd bought the horse, but—— As for Louise's other insinuations, those Matty could ignore and did. Jerry was no gambler. He had been, long ago, but he'd reformed before he even met Maisie. The fact was Louise didn't like Jerry any more than she liked Matty herself.

'My sister should never have married him,' she'd told Matty long ago, only months after Matty's mother had died and Jerry had taken her on as his responsibility. 'He's about as reliable as quicksand. Oh, I know he's a bookie and bookies generally do all right for themselves, but Jerry Bridle's a compulsive gambler— I know the type. He'll crash one of these days and then he'll expect to live on us. I don't know what Maisie sees in him—he's not our sort at all.'

Matty had been thirteen then, and it had hurt to hear this unfair criticism of the uncle who was the only living relative she had, and who had been so kind to her. But she was in no position to talk back to Louise. *She* was living on her in a way, she supposed. Jerry and Maisie didn't have a house of their own. Before he came over to the West, Jerry had been a horse-breaker in Queensland, where, as a child, Matty had lived with her parents. She remembered him as a rather colourful figure, visiting Glenna Downs, her father's small but prosperous cattle run on the Darling Downs. He was mad on horse racing in those days, and he was a heavy gambler. But when he left Queensland and shifted to Western Australia he turned over a new leaf. He took out a licence to operate as a bookmaker outside the metropolitan area, met Maisie, and gave up gambling altogether. Matty's mother had been very happy about it all—and reassured when she herself met Maisie.

'Even if she's not exactly out of the top drawer,' Matty remembered her saying with a laugh, 'she's a warm-hearted, very likeable woman, and she'll keep Jerry on an even keel, Treasure.'

That was when they had gone to Western Australia the year after Matty's father was killed in an accident. Glenna Downs had been sold and the money invested, and financially Matty and her mother had no worries. Grace Segal had intended buying a house in Perth and settling there, where she would be able to see something of her brother and his wife. But during their stay in Perth she had become ill and was rushed to hospital. Jerry had carried Matty off from the hotel where they'd been staying and installed her at Pepper-tree Lodge, in Maisie's care. Mrs Segal had died a few days later, after naming Jerry as Matty's guardian, and after that Peppertree Lodge was Matty's permanent home.

Louise didn't welcome her, but Maisie did—with open arms. And Jerry saw to it that she lived as her mother would have wished, to the best of his ability. She was enrolled at an exclusive school for girls, and while Jerry was away at the provincial races, which was most of the year, Maisie, childless, took a loving inter-est in her. Louise was the fly in the ointment. A rather big fly, full of unpleasant and often unnecessary com-plaints.

'Oh yes, you have everything you want, haven't you, with your famous inheritance,' she'd say to Matty. 'But it might occur to you one day that I'm the one who's making sacrifices for you. That double room you occupy—a mere kid—that room meant money to me before you were foisted on me.'

A child had no answer to such taunts—always made

when she was alone—and Matty was miserable at such times. A fact that had been largely responsible for her disastrous adventure with Patrick Dean, an adventure of which neither Jerry nor Maisie, both of them away at the time, had ever learned ...

Matty, busy making up her face in a hotel bedroom some seventeen hundred miles from Perth, had only half her mind on what she was doing. Her wandering thoughts returned to Jerry. After Louise's disturbing remarks about his health and his finances, she had known she'd have to go up for the Kurranulla round after all. She could help him the way Maisie liked to do, steady him. And if he was in financial trouble— well, there might be something she could do about that too. She had soon found an older woman willing to take her place at Peppertree Lodge, though she wasn't to take over the accounts, of course, and she told Louise firmly that she was taking time off, and that was that.

Even now, she didn't believe Jerry was drinking, though. She knew he must miss Maisie badly, but it was seven months since she had died, and without flattering herself Matty knew it meant something to Jerry that he still had her. When he had met her plane in Derby, she'd been distressingly aware that he was looking his age. New, deeper lines had joined the creases of good humour on his craggy face, but what had caused them she didn't yet know.

She found a bright lipstick that toned with the flame of her shirt and applied it generously. She was glad she'd come up here. Her personal apprehensions didn't really matter. The thing was, she'd be with Jerry for a few weeks and in that time, if he had any specific problems, then surely they could work out some kind of a solution together. It was not as if she were penniless!

A few minutes later she closed the door of the hotel

bedroom behind her and was on her way to look for Jerry.

Outside, the hot air hit her mercilessly, and she was thankful she'd rejected at least the black jeans. Even so, she was going to boil to death. The main street of the tiny town, that boasted, apart from a hotel, a post office and a garage, only a few dozen dwellings, was crammed with dusty cars. All along the footpath, in the shade of the trees that lined both sides of the street, groups of men in wide-brimmed hats stood talking. Yes, people certainly came into town during race week from hundreds of miles around. The unpalatable thought came back into Matty's mind once again, and she turned away from its implications. She was nervous enough already, and her smile wavered as she encountered the curious and interested glances of various tall tanned countrymen. She quailed at the thought of the crowd there'd be out at the racecourse when she went there presently with Jerry, in that handsome dark red car of his that had already carried her the dusty miles from Derby.

She found her uncle presently, standing in the shade of a baobab talking to another man.

'Oh, there you are, Treasure,' he greeted her as she joined them. 'You're looking very cool and eye-catching.'

Matty grimaced at the word. 'I'm feeling a bit *too* eye-catching!'

'Not a bit of it, you look beautiful,' Jerry said comfortingly. He turned to the man with him—fortyish, with a lean weatherbeaten face that made even Jerry look a little soft. 'Jim, this is my young niece, Matty Segal. I want her to see what great folk the people of the North-West are—the best in the world. Matty, meet Jim Travers. He runs the garage in town and he's always my clerk when I'm here.'

Matty smiled and Jim Travers smiled, and they all

moved over to Jerry's car. Jim sat in the front with Jerry, and as they drove out of town he turned around, his arm along the back of the seat, and looked at Matty.

'I've just been telling Jerry that they're having guests out at Bunda Bunda cattle station homestead during race week. I reckon I can wangle you an invitation, Matty—there's a shortage of girls in the North-West. They're having a bit of a do tomorrow night—lots of people. How about it?'

'You'd like it, Matty—you'd really like it,' Jerry put in as the car sped along the dusty road.

Matty's heart had begun to beat fast. She realised she was supposed to be pleased, but what if Bunda Bunda turned out to be Dirk Reasoner's cattle station?

She said with nervous brightness, 'But I—I don't know the people there. They mightn't like a stranger in their home.'

'Don't worry—they'll like you all right,' Jim said laconically. 'Their name's Fitzroy and they've been up here for donkey's years. I'll see you meet Lance this afternoon—and his sister too, with a bit of luck.'

Matty had relaxed. 'And Jerry?' she asked more easily, because after all she'd come here to be with her uncle—to find out if all was well with him. 'Will he be invited too?'

There was a tiny but slightly odd silence before Jerry said over his shoulder, 'I couldn't come, Treasure. I have things to keep me in town between now and Saturday. But if you have the chance, you go along. That's the whole idea of your being here—to meet people and enjoy yourself.'

'Okay,' said Matty. She wasn't altogether sure she should go. Still, if Jerry was going to be busy in town, she wouldn't see all that much of him—she might even be a nuisance. And they had a few weeks ahead of them, after all. She felt just a little bit excited at the thought of visiting a cattle station too. She'd be able to do some riding! She hadn't ridden a horse since she and her mother had left Glenna Downs, and that was a long time ago. Of course the cattle properties here wouldn't be in the least like her father's place on the Darling Downs, but she felt an odd touch of nostalgia. And so long as it wasn't Dirk Reasoner's station that Jim had plans of getting her an invitation to visit, she was quite happy. *That* was one place she'd avoid like the plague, though if Dirk Reasoner had any say in the matter—and of course he would have, seeing he was the big boss, as Patrick had told her four years ago—then she'd never in a million years be invited there.

She shivered involuntarily. It was no use trying to hide facts away in the back of her mind for ever. It was very much on the cards that she'd run into Dirk Reasoner in the near future, even though she didn't know exactly where he ran his cattle. Patrick, she remembered vaguely, had talked about Ridge Creek, and that was only a couple of hundred miles away. If Dirk Reasoner wasn't at Kurranulla, then he was very likely to turn up the following week at the Ridge Creek racecourse. And after that, there was still Wanganup. No, she couldn't really hope to avoid him altogether, unless he was as determined as she was, and refused to see her.

But if it did happen, what would she do?

She'd ignore him, she thought. She'd act as if she'd never seen him in her life.

The thought suddenly occurred to her that he might have forgotten her. Oh, how she hoped he had! How she hoped he would look at her just as blankly as she intended to look at him. There was not a single doubt in her mind that she'd recognise him—on sight! She'd met him only once, four years ago in Perth, in his own apartment. But she didn't even have to close her eyes to see again that threatening dark face, those white lines of anger drawn down from the nostrils, the contempt in the hard black eyes that branded her as being something she wasn't.

It was strange in a way that her feelings towards him were so much more intense than anything she felt for his very much younger half-brother, Patrick Dean. She couldn't even visualise Patrick as clearly as she could Dirk, despite the fact she'd met Patrick several times—though never, oddly enough, since that fateful night. His ambition in those days, when he was seventeen, had been to get away from Perth and go to his brother's cattle station. He had talked to her about that.

Matty drew a deep shuddering breath. 'Stop it,' she told herself fiercely, aware that she was shrinking back into herself, wishing she was hundreds of miles away, back in the safety of Peppertree Lodge, up to her ears in the bookwork, the menus, the counting of household linen. But the things that Dirk Reasoner had said to her when she was fifteen had left a scar on her that hadn't healed yet.

That, and not the fact that she was tied up with work at the private hotel, was the reason why Matilda Segal's life had been devoid of boy-friends. That was why she hadn't wanted to come to the North-West.

'Forget it,' she told herself again as her uncle pulled up the car in the shade of some trees at the racecourse. 'Pretend you're happy—wear a smile—get those punters flocking to Jerry's stand.'

It was a pretty racecourse. The grass was green and there were palm trees and baobabs and eucalypts to provide much-needed shade. In open-sided shelters, racegoers were picnicking still, and another shelter formed a bar where cans of beer were kept cold in great bins of ice. Jim Travers and Jerry introduced her to a number of people after they left the car—Matty hadn't a hope of keeping all their names in her head, and for a while she was absorbed, watching the horses, watching the country people—the men in hats with wide brims, the women in their best clothes, the young people cool-looking and fashionable. As for herself, she knew she was conspicuous in her rather theatrical clothes, and she knew too that a lot of men couldn't keep their eyes off her. Some came along to be introduced, some kept their distance, though they looked at her so hard she couldn't help being aware of it. They looked at her bare legs above the tops of the black boots, and they looked again. The women were different. Some raised their eyebrows and glanced away, others gave her a good-natured smile—and to them Matty was grateful.

Jerry, she discovered presently, had drawn the stand nearest the bar, which meant, he told her, that he'd get a lot of the small punters who left their beer drinking to place a small bet at the last minute, without bothering to see where they'd get the best odds.

'Is that good?' Matty asked, joining him and watching with interest as he set up his board with the names of the horses, and, on a roller section at the side, the odds he was offering. He wore a big money bag around his neck with 'Jerry Bridle' on it and his registration number.

'Oh, the bar trade's nothing much,' he said. 'It's the big punters who count, so it doesn't really matter which stand you draw.'

'Can you—lose a lot of money?' she asked after a moment. 'I mean, can a bookie lose a lot?' Jim wasn't there and she spoke quickly and anxiously.

'Well, not many bookies go broke,' Jerry grinned. 'What makes you ask me, Matty? Do I act like I'm down and out?'

She shook her head. 'No, of course not. I just wondered. I mean,' she floundered on, 'I know it was bad for you when you lost Sunshooter, and I just—I suppose I really wondered if—if you make a *lot* as a bookie, that's all,' she finished with a nervous laugh.

He gave her a sharp look. 'You don't need to worry about me, Treasure. What's up? Has Louise been putting the wind up you?'

Matty relaxed slightly. 'A little, I suppose.'

'Well, forget it—enjoy yourself,' Jerry told her.

She said no more, but watched him putting up the names of the horses in the first race and presently asked, 'What happened to that horse you sold a year ago, Jerry—Waltzing Matilda? Does she still run in the provincial races?'

'Not these days. That little mare's with a trainer in Perth now—she runs in the metropolitan races. She's done well this year—she's a winner.'

'Who owns her now?' Matty asked, and, curiously, she seemed through some crazy sixth sense to know the answer even before Jerry gave it.

'Dirk Reasoner from Moonak Station. He's here today—I saw him go over to the parade ring a few minutes ago. Why don't you go along and introduce yourself? Anyone'll point him out to you, and he knows me. He's a great bloke—I'd like you to meet him.'

Matty had turned away, her cheeks pale, panic rising in her nauseatingly. So he was here. She had only to go over to the parade ring and she'd see him . . .

'I'll stay here and help you, Jerry,' she said huskily. 'Like—like Maisie used to do.'

He stared at her and scowled.

'Now what's all this? You'll do nothing of the sort— I didn't bring you here to put you to work. I know you're good at figures, but Jim's my clerk. No, Matty, you run off. Have a bit of a flutter on the horses. Dirk Reasoner will tell you what to back—he'll be pleased to.'

Jim appeared then, before Matty could think of

anything to say, and after a moment she decided there was nothing for it but to do as Jerry had said. Or to pretend to. She smiled at both the men and moved away, her head lowered slightly so that the big curly brim of the black hat shaded her face. She knew she couldn't escape being noticed, dressed as she was in her bright shirt and white shorts, plus the black boots and hat. But instead of going to the small fenced-off enclosure where the horses to run in the next race were to be seen parading, she walked off in the opposite direction, got clear of the crowd and stood leaning against the white rails that ran round the race-track.

Her muscles, her nerves, were tense. She stood there for some minutes, staring at the green grass, trying to cast Dirk Reasoner out of her mind, telling herself that it didn't matter one way or the other whether she saw him or not. Ludicrously, she wished she were wearing her white dress, not this theatrical and ostentatious outfit. She wasn't going to be any use attracting punters to Jerry's stand. He didn't want her around, that was obvious. And though with a little tuition she might have been capable of acting as his pay-out clerk, she knew he didn't want that either. She was superfluous.

As for Dirk Reasoner——

With sudden decision she turned her back on the race-track and with her head high set off for the parade ring. She might as well get it over and done with. Then she could put it all behind her, relax, forget him.

He was there.

She saw him the minute she reached the rails. In fact, she looked across and found him with an immediate and deadly accuracy that was quite frightening. Big and dark and aggressive, he wore black pants, a black shirt—a green neckerchief that gave a dash, a glitter to his ruggedness. He wore no hat and his face looked deeply bronzed and his hair black in the fierce sunlight. She had thought him ugly four years ago. Now she was far from sure about that, though certainly from this distance his slightly crooked nose—it must have been broken at some time—was unnoticeable.

He was rolling a cigarette and listening, a slight frown on his face, to something the girl beside him was saying—a fair-haired girl whose face was half hidden by big sunglasses.

Matty's heart had given a great plunging movement in her breast and then begun to hammer. He was as she remembered him—yet not entirely. That early morning in Perth he'd worn a white shirt, the collar unbuttoned, his tie loosened, and he'd looked at least partly civilised. Here, in this crowd of country people, in the harsh sunlight, he took on a new dimension. He looked the sort of man who would take vengeance ruthlessly, who would use violence without hesitation to get what he wanted. He looked a man who could handle anything—and anyone. Without velvet gloves.

She swallowed, her throat dry. She was being over-fanciful. But he hadn't handled her with velvet gloves four years ago. Her hand went to her hat, to ease it a little away from her perspiring forehead. Her hair was damp, and she felt sick. She wanted to creep away, to disappear. She'd seen him, and the very sight of him had rocked her. It was no use telling herself she could behave coolly, look through him as if she didn't know him. She couldn't and—oh, she hated him!

She didn't know how long she stood there transfixed, aware with only the very edge of her mind of the handsome horses that were being led around the enclosure, of the jockeys in their bright silks and white breeches. It might have been minutes and it might have been no more than a few seconds, but she felt a new and deeper shock when, without even changing his position, he simply raised his eyes from the cigarette he'd been rolling and looked straight across at her—exactly as if he knew she was there.

'Look through him,' she told herself desperately. 'Look cool, look haughty—look as if you don't want to know.' But her mouth had begun to tremble and the colour came rushing to her cheeks. He didn't smile at her—well, had she ever thought he'd smile at Matilda Segal?—and yet she knew positively that he'd recognised her, despite the big hat, and the extreme unlikelihood of her appearing in this part of the world at all. It was only with a most determined effort of will that she stopped her thoughts from careering madly into a replay of what had happened four years ago, and kept her head up—to show him—oh, to show him what? She didn't really know. Because as far as she remembered—and she remembered every little detail —she couldn't show him anything. Not about Matty Segal. He'd made up his mind—he'd judged her, branded her——

At that moment someone touched her arm.

'Matty Segal?'

The spell was broken. She turned unsteadily to find herself confronting a tall laconic man of forty or so.

'Enjoying watching the horses? They're a pretty sight, aren't they? I suppose you want to make a bet. I favour Cap Fitz—the chestnut, number four. As you've probably guessed, it's owned by Brian Fitzroy.'

Matty was looking at him doubtfully. She was thankful in a way for being rescued, as it were, but who was this man? She supposed she must have met him earlier on, but——

'You've forgotten my name, haven't you?' he said quizzically. 'Jim introduced us a while ago and I spotted you here just now, all by yourself. I'm Don Graham. Do you remember now?'

'Oh—er—yes,' Matty said, though she didn't really, and he grinned.

'You don't,' he said. 'Well, I guess I'd have to be ten years younger to make an impression. I'm the overseer from Bunda Bunda. Maybe that rings a bell ... Anyhow, come along if you want to make a bet.'

'I should—I should go over with my uncle and Jim Travers,' Matty protested.

'Oh, eyewash! They don't want you there—you'd only be in the way. Besides, all the blokes would forget about the horses when they got an eyeful of you.'

Matty crimsoned. 'I shouldn't have worn shorts.'

'Oh, go on! You look beaut. You have the right sort of legs for shorts. Most of the women here would give their eye teeth to be able to dress like that, so if you've been getting any snooty looks, put it down to plain green-eyed jealousy. My wife thinks you look great, anyhow. We'll find her presently—she wants to meet you. She's somewhere around with the kids. Three of them,' he added with a happy grin.

He was nice, Matty thought, and she began to feel at her ease with him. She trotted off with him quite happily without a backward glance, and five minutes later she met his wife, Marie, and the three small boys, aged, they soon told her, five, seven and ten. Marie was plump, good-natured and a little homely, and from the minute she met her Matty began to enjoy herself. The Graham children rapidly attached themselves to her, and because she wasn't really interested in betting, she was happy to wander round with them. They stopped to stare at the horses and jockeys, to watch the races, to stand back and look at the crowds of people. The children chattered endlessly. They were having a week off from correspondence lessons, and they told her all about 'school', down by the rails near the race-track.

Later she went back with them to one of the picnic
shelters, because they were thirsty, and so was she, and
she found herself in the midst of a crowd of country
folk, most of them women and children—drinking tea
poured from Thermos flasks, filling plastic mugs with
home-made lemonade for the children. A few men
wandered in and out, but to Matty's relief Dirk
Reasoner didn't appear. In fact she hadn't seen him
since she'd moved away with Don Graham, and she suspected *he* might very well be partly to blame for that.

Then Lance Fitzroy from Bunda Bunda came in,
and after offering him a cup of tea, Marie introduced
him to Matty. She knew at once that he was interested
in her, as she sat with her booted legs crossed, bare
from below the knee to well up the thigh. He drank
his tea, eyeing her now and again. He was a few years
older than she was, very sure of himself, very well
dressed in light grey trousers, white shirt and a dark
red tie, and his tan shoes were well polished. He had
blue eyes and a smooth face, and Matty thought he
carried a little too much weight for his height, which
was medium.

Everyone was drifting away, and the shelter that had
been full of noisy kids and chattering women quietened
down. Apart from Matty and Lance, there were only a
few women packing up their picnic baskets, and exchanging a few remarks. Matty felt somehow nervous.
She would have liked to disappear too, but the
Graham children had taken off with friends, and she
stayed where she was, conscious that Lance Fitzroy was
taking very interested stock of her—and wishing that
he wasn't. She looked at him uneasily through her
lashes, and felt quite positive it was her showy clothes
that attracted him to her. She wanted to tell him,
'This isn't really me—I hate being noticed.'

'You've come up for the round, I suppose,' he said

after a long time, and it seemed to Matty he'd made a decision.

'Yes. I—we're staying at the hotel in town.'

'We?' he queried, his fair eyebrows cocked.

'My uncle and I,' she said. 'He's a bookmaker—Jerry Bridle.'

A curious look passed over his face and he frowned slightly. 'Jerry Bridle's your uncle?' he said unnecessarily.

'Yes. Do you know him?'

'Not personally,' said Lance with a slight and patronising smile. He continued abruptly, 'We're having a house party at Bunda Bunda. How about coming to stay till the Saturday race meeting? Or do you have something else lined up?'

Matty had nothing at all lined up, but Jim had said he'd try to wangle her an invitation to Bunda Bunda. She wondered if it had somehow or other been wangled through Marie Graham, and she asked curiously, 'Did Marie ask you to invite me?'

'Marie? Don't be silly—*I* want you to come.' His blue eyes left her face and travelled to her bosom and then to her bare thighs and her high-heeled boots. Matty felt the colour come into her face. She wasn't used to dealing with men of Lance's age, and she felt foolishly inhibited. She felt herself go cold inside so that she wanted to run away, to disappear. Which was ridiculous. After all, she was being invited to a house party. It would be fun, she told herself firmly. Jerry would want her to go, to meet people, to enjoy herself. Not to hang around like a wet blanket. She forced a bright smile.

'Thank you, then. It would be very nice. So long as my uncle——'

'Oh, your uncle won't have any objections,' Lance assured her. 'He'll think it's a bit of a step up the

ladder for his niece to be invited to our place, anyway.'
He got up from the bench where he'd been sitting and
smiled down at her. 'I'll fix it up with the parents and
arrange transport for you. You'll be eating dinner at
the hotel, I presume.'

'Yes,' Matty nodded.

'Good. Then I'll see you later.'

He strode off and she stared after him perplexedly.
Was she being—patronised? That remark about a step
up the ladder—— She wasn't altogether sure she wanted
to go to the Fitzroys' house party. After all, she'd only
just met Lance, so why had he invited her? She thought
of the way he had looked at her, and then she remembered Jim had said there was a shortage of girls in the
North-West. So *that* was why . . .

During the rest of the afternoon she saw nothing
more of Lance, and she finally reached the conclusion
he hadn't been able to 'fix it up' with his parents.
Either they didn't want any more guests, or they didn't
want a stranger in their midst. Either way, Matty
didn't really care. She found the Graham children and
forgot the whole thing.

When the races were over she went back to the hotel
with her uncle, took a shower and changed into a
sleeveless peach-coloured dress with a round neckline,
and clasped a white opal pendant round her throat.
After she'd brushed out her shining, newly washed
hair and applied a little make-up, she joined her uncle
in the dining room. She'd said nothing about the invitation to Bunda Bunda, but Jerry asked about it
himself, as they ate their steaks and salad.

'I guess you met the Fitzroys, Treasure. Anything
doing?'

Matty made a wry face. 'I met Lance, that's all, and
if you mean was I invited to their house party—well,
I was, but Lance said he'd have to see his parents first,

and that's the last I heard of it. Perhaps they haven't got room for another guest.'

Jerry's pleasant mouth tightened. 'They're not short of space,' he said flatly. 'You should have mentioned that your father used to own Glenna Downs, then they'd have shown a little interest.'

Matty looked surprised, then shrugged. 'Don't worry, Jerry. I don't mind, and anyhow, I'll be perfectly happy staying here in town with you.'

'I didn't ask you here for that,' Jerry said obstinately. 'The whole idea is for you to meet people—get around. If young Fitzroy's so ill-mannered as to give you an invitation and then renege, he can go to hell. I'll guarantee Dirk Reasoner wouldn't behave in that cavalier fashion. When we move on to Ridge Creek I'll get you an invitation there.'

Matty felt herself go red and then white, and she bit her lip. It was no use Jerry planning to have her asked to visit Dirk Reasoner's home. She wouldn't go —and in any case, if Jerry only knew it, there wasn't one chance in a million she'd ever be invited there.

She said quickly, 'Jerry, please! I don't want to—to visit people on their cattle stations. I'm not a good mixer——'

'And that's because you've been a prisoner at Louise's hotel ever since you left school,' her uncle said vehemently. 'You don't meet any young folk there. I should never have let it happen—I've been a fool. It would have been different if Maisie were still alive— if you and she had had that trip to Europe. I've made an absolute hash of bringing you up—your mother should never have trusted you to me. My God, you should have had flocks of young men around you, a pretty girl like you. You should have had half a dozen proposals by now, and don't tell me marriage is out of date, either. It's certainly not so up here in the outback, at any rate, and if you want to know, that's one good reason for your being here—to meet some decent men, to give you a chance of finding a suitable husband.'

Matty was quivering slightly. Her uncle was getting so worked up that his face was growing red, and she put a hand on his arm.

'Jerry, don't get so upset about it! I assure you I have nothing against marriage, but there's no hurry—I'm not quite twenty yet! And don't say you've made a hash of looking after me. I haven't minded helping Aunt Louise. I do owe her something, you know, and it's not as if I need do it for ever, is it?—even if I don't get married.' She was thinking that when she was twenty-one she'd be free to do as she chose with the money left her by her mother, and she knew it would be considerable, because Glenna Downs had been a valuable property. She knew that all her living expenses, her school fees and so on had been paid for out of the interest on the investments, but as Jerry had handled it all she'd never needed to worry about it.

'What do you think I should do, Jerry?' she asked now. 'When I turn twenty-one, I mean.'

Her uncle's frown deepened. 'We'll have to talk about that some time Matty,' he said rather heavily. 'There are—things you'll have to know, and I've been meaning to get around to it, but——'

He broke off in mid-sentence, and glancing round, Matty saw that Don Graham was crossing the room towards them.

'Hello there, Jerry—Matty. I just dropped in to see if Matty can be ready in about half an hour. I've left Marie and the kids at the Travers' place—we've been having a meal with Jim and his wife.'

'You're taking Matty out to Bunda Bunda with you?' Jerry exclaimed enthusiastically. 'Good! We were wondering what was going on.' His frown had vanished and he was looking good-humoured once again, and Matty wished she could match his enthusiasm. He obviously had his heart set on having her meet eligible men, though why on earth he should have got it into his head that it was time she thought about marriage, she didn't know, and the fact was, she didn't really want to go to Bunda Bunda at all.

'We've just about finished dinner, Don,' Jerry was saying. 'Matty can easily be ready in half an hour—can't you, Treasure?'

'Yes, but I really don't think I——' Her voice trailed away. There was that worried look back on her uncle's face. It looked as if she'd have to go just to please him. She'd evidently misjudged Lance Fitzroy, however—he had fixed things up with his parents. He had merely failed to let her know what arrangements had been made. She looked up at Don Graham and forced a smile.

'I'll be ready when you are, Don,' she said.

A few minutes later she was in her room packing. She wouldn't take everything with her—she'd brought a whole heap of clothes. She could leave one of her suitcases in Jerry's room.

She packed quickly. Two pairs of jeans—everyone wore jeans, and she might get a chance to go riding—two or three good shirts. Her swimsuit—a modest one-piece. Her white shorts needed laundering after today, so she couldn't take those. Instead she included her white dress, and for evening wear she chose a rather unusual gown of black and tan silk, because there was supposed to be a party tomorrow night. She'd brought three evening outfits with her, all of them new, because she knew that various social events were held during race week in the different towns, and she remembered Maisie always took clothes to 'dress up in'. She'd wear the dress she had on now; it would be suitable for dinner provided the Fitzroys weren't too formal. She thought inconsequently of what Jerry had said about Glenna Downs, but she wasn't going to upgrade herself by mentioning that. It didn't make any difference to what she was, anyhow, and right now she was Matilda Segal who worked in a private hotel in Perth, and was just now on a visit to the North-West with her bookmaker uncle. It was funny in a way—she didn't really know who she was, what kind of a girl she was. She hadn't had much opportunity to find out since she'd left school. She knew she'd made a mistake in wearing those shorts today, and at the back of her mind was a suspicion that Lance had judged her by her clothes. He had such an air of superiority—and he'd really thought she'd snap up his invitation eagerly.

If she'd been dressed more conventionally, Matty thought, he mightn't have been so casual. He'd have settled everything before he'd let her out of his sight—and he'd have taken her to meet his parents and his sister. Obviously he didn't judge her as the kind of girl worthy of such consideration. 'I like the country folk,' she remembered hearing Maisie say once, to Louise. 'But all the same, I reckon some of them think they're a superior breed to us city people. I suppose it's because they've pioneered the land or something. Oh well, good luck to them, they're no happier than I am, anyway—I know that.'

Matty carried her suitcase downstairs with a feeling of apprehension. She wasn't looking forward to this visit to Bunda Bunda.

CHAPTER TWO

THE fifty-kilometre drive to the Fitzroys' cattle station was a little rough, but not uncomfortably so. The night air seemed agreeably cool after the hot day, and the three Graham boys were soon asleep in the back of the station wagon. Marie and Don discussed the races, the horses—particularly the horse from Bunda Bunda station—and passed on to each other news they'd picked up from various country people.

'I suppose Lance told you they're having a bit of a party at the homestead tomorrow night,' Marie asked Matty presently.

'No, he didn't mention it. But Jim told me earlier, so I've packed a dress.'

'That's fine,' said Marie. 'I couldn't have loaned you one of mine—it'd be a mile too big for you. You'd swim in anything belonging to Rona, too—she's a lot bigger build than you.'

Rona. Rona Fitzroy. There'd been a girl of that name at Matty's school—a boarder, and three years or so senior to Matty.

'Is that Lance's sister?' she asked curiously.

'Yes. Didn't you meet her?'

'I didn't meet any of them ... Will you and Don be coming to the party, Marie?'

'I shouldn't think so. But Lance will give you a good time. Are you interested, by the way?'

'What do you mean?' Matty couldn't see Marie's face in the darkness—the three adults were sitting in the side front seat—but she could hear the amused surprise in the other woman's voice as she exclaimed,

'In Lance, of course! He's a very eligible bachelor

—and of course you know men outnumber girls in this part of the world.'

'Marie!' Don exclaimed reprovingly. 'Cut it out—Matty's only here to enjoy herself, not to look for a husband.'

'Don't be so literal, Don. She mightn't be looking for a husband, but every girl knows that any day she might meet the man she's destined to marry. That's romance. Or have you met him already, Matty?' she asked laughingly when Matty was silent. 'Down south, I mean.'

'No, there's—there's no one,' Matty answered.

'I didn't think so. You look too young, anyhow. How old are you?'

'Not so very young. I'm nearly twenty. But I'm *not* looking for a husband,' Matty hastened to add. 'I don't want to get married for ages.'

'That's what I said,' Marie said with a laugh. 'Then Don came along, and here I am—thirty-one, with three great big kids and a hungry husband.'

'And don't you love it!' Don teased.

Despite everything, Matty found it exciting to see the homestead lights appear in a darkness that had before been almost complete, and in no time Don was slowing down.

'We'll see you later, I hope,' Marie said warmly, as he pulled up outside the gate, and Matty agreed that she hoped so too.

Don took her suitcase and escorted her through the garden and on to the verandah, which was tiled, and made attractive by an array of pot-plants, some of them in flower. From inside the house floated the sound of voices and of recorded music, and as Don knocked loudly on the front door Matty felt a shiver of premonition touch her nerves. She wished Jerry were here too—and she wished she didn't have this hang-up about visiting people. She hoped Lance wouldn't be so casual about welcoming her as he had been over the arrangements for getting her here. At least she was looking more presentable than she had this afternoon, now she was in her pretty dress, over which she'd slipped a silk-knit ivory-coloured jacket.

It seemed a long time before anyone answered Don's knock, but at least it was Lance. And close behind him was a girl, with straight, shoulder-length blonde hair—the girl, Matty realised with an odd little shock, who had been with Dirk Reasoner this afternoon, watching the horses. Now, with her sunglasses off, she looked vaguely familiar, and Matty was almost certain she must be Rona Fitzroy.

'Here's your guest, Lance,' she heard Don say. 'Safely delivered and all in one piece ... Goodnight, Matty, we'll see you later.'

He had gone and Lance was smiling at her, but the girl with him was not. Her blue eyes looked coldly at Matty, who recognised her instantly as one of the outback people Maisie had mentioned—the ones who thought they were superior to city folk. She was like her brother in that she was blonde and blue-eyed— and also in that she was a little overweight, though certainly she looked very attractive in a long sea-green skirt and matching top.

Lance introduced the girls to each other—'My sister Rona—Matty Segal.' Even then Rona didn't smile, but merely looked at Matty superciliously.

'I saw you at the race meeting this afternoon in that big black hat and boots, and I thought you were a circus girl or something. Are you? *Is* there a circus in town?'

Matty flushed deeply, and waited in vain for Lance to explain who she was. 'I'm Jerry Bridle's niece,' she said at last.

'Jerry Bridle's niece!' Rona's voice expressed total incredulity, and she looked at her brother and raised her eyebrows and smiled unpleasantly. 'Well, I'll leave you to it, Lance. I don't know what sleeping arrangements have been made for Jerry Bridle's niece ... I'm going back inside.'

She turned on her heel and disappeared, and Matty looked at Lance, who had picked up her suitcase.

'Don't take any notice of Rona,' he said, putting an arm around her shoulders. 'You look fabulous, Matty —just like a peach. I could eat you.'

Matty managed a smile, though she didn't feel consoled. Rona's rudeness had been quite unconcealed, yet to make a scene about it would be both undignified and impolite. It was just one of those things you closed your eyes to—if you could. She knew this instinctively. All the same she was angry, and she told herself that when she had an opportunity, she might remark that she and Rona had attended the same school. It was quite an exclusive school, and it might make Rona Fitzroy think twice before she insulted Matty again.

'You can sleep in one of the rooms along here, Matty,' Lance told her, leading her along a side corridor that opened off the main hall. 'There are still a couple unoccupied—we've started using the verandah beds, actually, but we've got a few more guests arriving tomorrow.'

He opened a door and showed Matty in. It was a pretty bedroom with pale satin-striped wallpaper, light wood furniture, and soft furnishings in white and yellow with a touch of black. The bracket lights on the wall and over the mirror cast a soft light. It was a far prettier and more luxurious room than Matty had slept in since she had been a child at Glenna Downs—except for the hotel in Perth where she and her mother had stayed so brief a time—and she looked around her appreciatively. There were two beds, each of a comfortable size, and Lance put Matty's suitcase on the floor and watched her as she slipped out of her jacket and laid it on one of the beds.

'Well, now you're here——' said Lance, and paused, his eyes crawling over her. Matty could see in his face what he was going to do and stepped back instinctively, but he took her hard by her upper arms and pulled her against him, and reached for her mouth. She turned her head aside swiftly, smelling beer on his breath. 'Don't,' was all she managed to say before he had forced her head around and pressed his mouth against hers. She struggled against him, and felt him fumbling with the top of her dress—pulling the zipper at the back down until he'd loosened it enough to drag it down from one of her shoulders and slide his hand inside, his fingers greedy on her bare skin.

Her breath came fast. Hardly knowing what she was doing, she kicked him on the shin, and the unexpectedness of her action made him relax his hold momentarily. She twisted free of him and rushed straight for the door. Lance followed her, and his arms had encircled her waist from behind before she'd gone more than two yards along the hallway.

'Let me go!' she panted, and it was at that identical moment that a man appeared at the other end of the hall, only a few feet away. For a second he looked at the two of them—at Matty's disordered dress and bare shoulder, at the hands that pulled her close against the man behind her. Then, raising his dark eyebrows, he turned his back and retraced his steps.

Matty wished she could disappear through a hole in the ground. Dirk Reasoner! Oh God, she must be seeing things! He couldn't possibly be here at Bunda Bunda. Yet quite plainly he was—and he'd caught her out in a sexy skirmish with Lance Fitzroy ...

With a furious movement she wrenched herself away from Lance, who had actually started to nuzzle her shoulder. She straightened the top of her dress and raised her arms to pull up the zip fastener.

'How *dare* you!' she exclaimed on an angry sob. Lance was helping her with the zipper and she heard him laugh softly, but her expression as she whirled round sobered him, and he grimaced.

'I'm sorry, but how was I to know anyone would see us? You shouldn't have rushed out here, anyhow—no one would have interrupted us in the bedroom.'

Matty bit her lip. Did he think she enjoyed that sort of thing—wanted it? Of course she'd rushed out, to protect herself. His strength was vastly superior to hers. But for Dirk Reasoner to see it all—— Mentally, she wrung her hands in anguish. If she'd known he'd be here, she'd never have come herself. As it was, it appeared that her acceptance of his invitation meant, to Lance, an acceptance of his attentions. If it had been possible, she'd have picked up her suitcase and walked out. Maybe she could even do just that—find the Graham's bungalow, ask to stay there.

Yet even as she hurried back to the bedroom she knew she couldn't do it. Because what could she say? 'Lance tried to kiss me. Somebody saw us——' It was pathetic, it was laughable. And it was impossible.

Lance had followed her into the bedroom, and now he said, sounding slightly bored, 'You'd better comb your hair and I'll take you to meet my parents and the others.'

Matty shook her head violently. 'Just go away and leave me alone,' she said furiously.

'Oh, come on now, what's wrong? What are you trying to make out I've done?' He came closer and she stepped back, blinking away the angry tears that had come into her eyes. She was quite hopeless in a situation like this. She didn't know how to handle it, and she supposed Lance probably thought she was unbelievably prudish. She knew she'd have to pull herself together, because after all, he hadn't done anything, and she was well aware that what rankled was the fact that Dirk Reasoner had seen her struggling with Lance.

Lance spoke again, after a moment, but more moderately this time.

'I was only fooling, Matty. I wasn't going to do anything you didn't want ... Okay, I've had a few beers, so I unzipped you, and I'm sorry. I'll behave myself. Come on, smile—say you forgive me, and let's go and join the others.'

'All right.' Matty forced herself to say it, though her voice shook a little and she couldn't achieve a smile and didn't even try to. 'But there's one thing I want to say, Lance—I think you've got quite the wrong idea about me. I guess when you invited me here you had—other things in mind. *You* thought I looked like a circus girl this afternoon too, didn't you? Cheap and——'

'No, not cheap,' he protested uncomfortably. 'You're very pretty—I could really go for you. I don't care who your relations are.'

Matty stared at him. 'Meaning Jerry Bridle,' she said, her eyes bright. 'Well, let me tell you this—my uncle is a decent, honourable man, and I have a lot more respect for him than I have for you and your sister!' As she spoke, she found her comb and dragged it furiously through her hair. 'Now let's forget it. I'm here and there's nothing I can do about that. Take me to meet your parents.'

Her head high, she marched to the door and he followed her.

The sitting room was a big handsome room, beautified with great bowls of flowers. At one end, Lance's parents were playing bridge with the Simmonds, another middle-aged couple. Lance introduced Matty, and she was aware of a chilling indifference, and supposed wryly that the Fitzroys thought her socially inferior—as undoubtedly Rona and Lance did. Because of her get-up that afternoon, because of her uncle. Rona had doubtless told them about her uncle by now. It was almost a relief to leave them to their cards and go and meet the younger group—though there was still the ordeal of facing Dirk Reasoner.

Lance didn't make formal introductions. He simply announced that she was Matty Segal, then named the others in turn—Helen, Nerida and Stuart Simmonds, the jackeroo, Warwick Frost. Rona she had met already, and last of all there was Dirk Reasoner. Matty's legs felt like giving way when it came round to Dirk Reasoner. She was so shattered inwardly she could barely look at him. Crazily, she expected him to say, 'We've met before,' but he didn't. He smiled as distantly as if the introduction were a mere convention and they would never be expected to exchange another word with each other. And she hoped—oh, how she hoped—that they wouldn't. Though somehow she didn't think she was going to get off as lightly as that.

In another minute she was accepting a glass of chilled white wine from Lance, and then some of the others started dancing on the side verandah. Stuart Simmonds claimed Rona, Warwick carried off Nerida, a pretty teenager, and Helen, older than her sister, came over to Matty and Lance and said abruptly, 'Lance promised to dance with me next. I hope you don't mind.'

'Of course not,' Matty said nervously, and smiled back at Lance as he took Helen's arm automatically and disappeared with her. She glanced around her uneasily. Apart from the two couples playing bridge at the other end of the room, there were now only Dirk Reasoner and herself left. He was across the room, near the radiogram, and she looked at him through her lashes. Thank goodness he didn't feel obliged to ask her to dance. On the contrary, he was taking absolutely no notice of her. He wore dark pants and a cream cotton shirt with a roll neck, and he didn't even glance in her direction, but stood as though he were deep in thought, his brow slightly creased.

Matty sipped her drink and tried to persuade herself she was perfectly at her ease, but she wasn't. Her hand had begun to shake, and in desperation she swallowed down the rest of the wine and set the stemmed glass down with unintentional noisiness on a low table.

At the sound Dirk glanced over at her, and then, to her dismay, he left his position by the player and crossed the room towards her.

'Do you want another drink?' His voice was cool and level, and his eyes, now that he was closer to her, seemed to examine her mercilessly as if he wanted to discover what had become of her after four years.

'No, thank you,' she said carefully. She pushed back a tendril of hair from her forehead with a nervous hand, and suffered his regard. Several seconds passed during which neither of them said anything, and then, as though she couldn't help it, she looked up at him again. He was still looking at her, and their eyes met with a kind of deadly precision, and Matty felt a shock go through her. She stared transfixed into the blackness of his eyes and wondered if he was remembering what she was remembering. And she knew he was. He couldn't possibly not be remembering—that morning he had caught her naked in his flat in Perth, where Patrick, his seventeen-year-old half-brother, was still asleep in the only bed.

She'd crept into the living room for her clothes—it wasn't much past dawn—meaning to sneak away before Patrick woke. And then she'd heard a key in the door, and *he* had stepped inside.

It all leaped into her mind and she groped behind her and sat down weakly on the arm of a chair.

She'd had one bad shock already that morning—
waking with a splitting headache to find she'd spent
the night in Dirk Reasoner's flat, and that she was
wearing nothing—nothing at all. And that Patrick
Dean was asleep on the other side of the bed. Whatever it was she'd been drinking the previous night
must have knocked her out so completely she remembered nothing after being sick in the bathroom.

Dirk Reasoner's arrival, coming on top of all that,
had brought her to the most terrible moment in her
life.

The low-necked black dress she'd snatched up from
the sofa and dragged over her head had done nothing
but add to the impression she'd already made on him.
Later he'd called her a cheap little courtesan. And
she'd said, heart hammering, 'Who do you think you
are, to talk about people like that? You bring girls
here——'

'Not fifteen-year-old girls,' he'd said acidly, and
added to that, 'If Patrick wants sexual experience,
I'd sooner he got it from an older woman—or a
prostitute. Not from a schoolgirl.'

That was on the way to Peppertree Lodge, and when
they'd got there he'd asked Louise didn't she care if
Matty stayed out all night. Louise had merely shrugged
her plump shoulders.

'She's my sister's responsibility, not mine. I can't
stay up all night waiting for her to come in. If she gets
herself into trouble it's her own fault, she's hardly a
child at fifteen and she has an old head on her
shoulders. Besides, she's on the pill. They all are, these
days.'

'I'm not!' Matty had wanted to say, but she had
been too ashamed to say anything. All she'd wanted
was to live through it somehow and emerge with it all
behind her—forgotten. Louise had marched out of the

sitting room to see to her work, thus expressing complete indifference, and Dirk Reasoner had told Matty tersely, 'If you don't watch it, your pretty little air of innocence will have completely vanished before you're twenty, and you'll have the hard face of a harlot.' On that note he'd gone. She never knew what he said to Patrick, for she never saw Patrick again. As for Louise—— 'What were you up to last night, anyhow?' she'd asked, and Matty had lied and said that a whole group of kids from school had gone to one of the boy's homes after the concert—that they'd stayed up all night dancing and talking because his parents were away. And Louise had at least pretended to believe her . . .

'I said do you want to dance?' she heard Dirk Reasoner saying, and came back to her senses with a start.

'Not—with you,' she answered, her voice low and unsteady.

His dark brows rose a fraction, and she went on as though compelled, aware that the sound of the music prevented the bridge players from hearing what she was saying, 'I don't want to have anything to do with you. I don't like you. I haven't forgotten the things you said to me—not any of them.'

'I hope you haven't,' he said. 'I hope I frightened hell out of you.'

He watched her as she nervously smoothed her skirt over her knees, then his eyes strayed upwards to linger on the neck of her dress and she felt ice at her nerve ends. He was thinking how he'd caught her in the hall with Lancc. She felt sick.

He sat down on the sofa opposite her and began to roll a cigarette.

'What are you doing in the North-West, anyhow?'

'What do you think?' she retorted. 'I came up for

the Kurranulla round. With my uncle, Jerry Bridle,'
she added deliberately. 'You probably know him. He's
a bookie.'

She saw a brief flash of surprise light his face. 'Jerry
Bridle's your uncle? I didn't know that.'

'I don't suppose you did. I hope you don't mind,'
she added ironically, looking straight at him.

Dirk ignored that. He ran his tongue down the edge
of the cigarette paper, finished making the cigarette
without looking at it, tucked in a few stray ends of
tobacco and asked her, 'Do you want a smoke?'

'No, thank you.'

'I bought a horse from your uncle not so long ago,'
he said next. 'Waltzing Matilda.'

'I know,' Matty said coldly. 'She was named for me.
My uncle bought her when she was a yearling. He
shouldn't have sold her.'

He gave her a tilted smile. 'To me, do you mean?
Well, I didn't twist his arm. He sold the horse because
he needed the money. His wife and daughter wanted a
trip to Europe, I believe.'

Matty flinched. 'My uncle hasn't got a daughter.
And he—he didn't want the money for that.'

His eyebrows rose sardonically. 'No? What's your
story, then?'

'I don't have a story. I don't know why he sold her.
I just know for a fact it wasn't for that. Because it was
—I was the one who was going to Europe with my
aunt.'

He smiled slightly. 'Did you enjoy your trip?'

'We didn't go. My aunt died in April this year—
she'd been ill.'

'I'm sorry.' He said it flatly, formally, and there was
a brief silence before he asked her, 'What are you
doing with yourself these days? You must have left
school——'

'Yes—at the end of last year. I—I work at a private

hotel. I do the accounts and lots of odds and ends.'

'I see. And how did you get here?'

'Here? I came with my uncle,' she said, not quite following him. Her senses were swimming. It was partly the wine, partly that the build-up of tension that had held her rigid had relaxed somewhat.

'I meant to Bunda Bunda. Tonight,' he said.

'Oh. Don Graham drove me out from Kurranulla ... Lance invited me here,' she added.

'He did?' Dirk sounded sceptical, and she felt herself flush, and put her hand to a pulse that had begun to hammer at her throat.

'Are you implying that I invited myself?'

'I'm not implying anything. I do know from the general reaction when Rona said you'd arrived that you weren't exactly—expected.'

Matty felt a surge of indignation. So Lance hadn't arranged anything with his parents—or perhaps they had made objections. It could be that with the extra guests who were expected tomorrow they already had a houseful, but she had an uneasy suspicion it was more than just that.

'Perhaps you'd better ask Lance whether he invited me here or not,' she said coldly.

'Oh, I'm not going to check up on you. I'm sure Lance wants you here, and anyhow it's nothing to do with me. Is it?' He hadn't lit his cigarette, but now he flicked on his lighter and gave her a very unnerving look across the flame. And this time she knew very well what was in his mind—that chase along the hall, her messed-up dress——

Suddenly unable to bear it any longer, Matty got up and walked away from him. The record hadn't ended, but Rona and Stuart had come in from the verandah. Rona looked at Matty angrily, then walked over to Dirk. Stuart, following her, smiled as he passed Matty and she smiled back and felt just fractionally better. If everyone—except Lance, who went to the other extreme—was going to give her the cold shoulder, then she simply couldn't face two and a half days here.

When Rona put another record on the player, Lance danced with Matty. In the half dark at the far end of the verandah his lips were against her hair and he held her close against him. It wasn't the way the others were dancing, and she hated it, and as soon as the dance was ended she told him, 'I'm going to bed, Lance. I'm tired.'

'Okay,' he said. He held her hand lingeringly as they went into the sitting room, then dropped it as she went purposefully to the other end of the room where her host and hostess were still playing bridge.

'Goodnight, Mr and Mrs Fitzroy—Mr and Mrs Simmonds,' she said clearly. 'Will you excuse me if I go to bed now? All those hours in the sun have made me sleepy.'

'Of course—go along—er——' said Mrs Fitzroy, obviously not remembering her name. 'Has Lance shown you where you can put your things?'

'Yes, thank you. In the bedroom with the white and yellow curtains. Is that all right? I know I'm an extra guest, and I don't want to upset your arrangements.'

Lance's father, a man with fading sandy hair and a complexion that was red rather than brown, had got to his feet, and when his wife, tight-lipped, said nothing, he told Matty, 'We won't let you do that. We've a big house here. I didn't catch you name, I'm afraid.'

'Matilda Segal,' said Matty, and added deliberately, 'I'm Jerry Bridle's niece.'

'Yes, so I believe,' Mr Fitzroy said. His wife was glaring at him, and the Simmonds were looking uncomfortable.

'It's terribly nice of you to allow me to come at such short notice,' Matty went on, with the idea of smoothing things over. She continued with a rush, 'I was at the same school as Rona, as a matter of fact, though she was two or three years ahead of me.'

'What?' Rona's supercilious voice floated across the room. 'You were at my school? I doubt it. I didn't know all the day girls, but Matilda Segal's hardly the sort of name one would forget, and I have no recollection of ever hearing it ... What school are we talking about, by the way?'

Matty looked straight at her as she named the school, then continued smoothly, 'It doesn't matter really. As you say, you were a boarder and I was a day girl. But I just thought I'd mention it.' She was aware that everyone was listening now, even though some of the others were standing around the record player, deciding what disc to play next. Dirk Reasoner was making no pretence of not listening, and he was watching Matty through narrowed eyes. He surely knew—from Patrick—what school she had gone to, yet he said nothing, and on a mad impulse Matty told Rona, 'You must remember those concerts we used to have in conjunction with the boys from the college nearby.'

Rona shrugged. 'That sort of thing's customary at most schools.' She looked bored, and turned abruptly to the others. 'Does anyone want coffee?'

Matty, for one, didn't. She had had enough of this, and with a murmured goodnight to anyone who might be listening, she crossed to the door.

Lance followed her and took her by the arm. 'Stay and have some supper Matty.'

She shook her head. Didn't he know she wasn't exactly enjoying herself? Did he think she was thick-skinned—brash?

'I'm going to bed, Lance.'

He spread his hands. 'Well, if you must.' Then, incredibly, 'Did you really go to the same school as Rona?'

'What do you think?' Matty said coldly, and turned away.

In her bedroom—the yellow and white room to which she knew she had no right—she stood, fists clenched, gritting her teeth. They were snobs, these outback people of whom Jerry had such a great opinion. Yet what was so wrong with Matty Segal? To display bad taste in dress—which she knew she had done—was that so very dreadful? And did having an uncle who was a bookmaker turn one into a social outcast? Matty gave up. She didn't care, anyhow, she told herself firmly.

But there was one thing she couldn't pretend not to care about, and that was Dirk Reasoner's presence here. It would do her no good if *he* aired his opinion of her. She stood staring at nothing, seeing his face, trying to compare it with the image that had burned at the back of her mind for the past four years. The same—yet different. He was—more attractive looking than she remembered, and much as she disliked him she couldn't deny it. Somehow he didn't look any older now than he had then, but perhaps that was because she had grown up. His eyes were still hostile, that was plain, and it was obvious he disliked her as much as she disliked him.

What did he see when he looked at her? she wondered. Did he think she'd hung on to her—her little-girl air of innocence? Did he imagine, after seeing her and Lance wrestling together tonight, that she was still a cheap little courtesan? She pressed her hands to her burning cheeks. Two more days, she thought, before she could go back to town.

She got ready for bed quickly, and lay longing for the oblivion of sleep. But sleep wouldn't come, and it was less the coolness of the Fitzroys than her encounter with Dirk Reasoner that troubled her. In her mind, she went over and over their brief conversation. She was puzzled by what he'd said about Waltzing Matilda. Why *had* Jerry sold the horse? Definitely he hadn't needed the money for that trip to Europe—that was to have been paid for out of Matty's investments, in accordance with her mother's wishes.

Well, she would have to remain in ignorance about that. It wasn't her part to question her uncle about his own business.

Her thoughts turned to Patrick. He couldn't be working on Dirk's cattle station, she decided, or she'd have been sure to have seen him at the races.

Patrick . . .

Exhausted though she was, her mind turned back to the trail it had been following earlier. To that night she had gone with Patrick Dean to Dirk's flat, in Perth.

The evening had begun, in a way, so innocently. And yet she was forced to admit, not altogether innocently, because when she'd set out from Peppertree Lodge to go to the school concert she'd been in a mood of revolt against Louise. Maisie had been away with Jerry for nearly a month, and Louise, who had always resented her presence, had alternately ignored and nagged her. She was an unwanted encumbrance at any time, but with Maisie away doubly so.

'Why we ever had to be saddled with you, I don't know. You're not a relation—you never do a hand's turn. You're going to be rich—oh yes, Matty Segal will never have to work for a living! But meanwhile *I'm* the one who's sacrificing one of my best rooms—a double room—and you're paying practically nothing for it. If I were my sister, I'd tell Jerry Bridle to pack you off to boarding school and no nonsense. You'd be a good deal less nuisance there anyhow. With all the men we have coming and going here and your figure developing, anything could happen. No matter if most of our men are old enough to be your father, men are all the same, and God knows I don't have time to be playing nursemaid to you.'

It had gone on and on, and Matty had reached the point where she wanted to run away. She hated coming home from school in the afternoons. No matter how agreeable she was, how much she tried to help or to keep out of the way, she couldn't please Louise. That night, even though she wasn't particularly keen to go to the concert, she went—to get away from Louise. She had a new dress, a black one. She'd bought it the day before, out of the generous allowance Jerry gave her, to delay the time when she'd have to go home. And when she had put it on that night it was the cause of another row with Louise.

'It's downright ridiculous a girl of fifteen having a sophisticated expensive dress like that. All it does is make you look like a tart, if you want to know—all that bosom you're showing, and your little-girl face. You're asking for trouble. And if you get it,' she added spitefully, 'I just don't want to know. You can have it all on your own.'

Did she look like a tart? Matty didn't think so. The dress did have a low-cut neckline, but then it was a hot night. In her heart she knew very well that her dress was too old for her, and that it wasn't suitable to wear to a school concert. But she didn't care. She was in a reckless mood, so she rang for a taxi—an extravagance that Louise deplored—and off she went.

Quite by chance she had a seat next to Patrick Dean who, like her, was by himself. She'd met him a few times before, at other school functions, and she'd always thought him terribly good-looking with his dark hair and that rather brooding expression that somehow made him seem more mature, more exciting than other boys of his age. He'd never taken much notice of her, and she knew he had a reputation for being a bit wild. That night, during the concert, she felt his eyes on her several times, and then in low tones they began exchanging views on the various musicians who were entertaining them. Some of Patrick's remarks were decidedly uncomplimentary and made her giggle under her breath. When the concert was over he asked if her parents were picking her up.

'I have to get a taxi,' she'd told him.

'Don't bother, I'll take you hame. I have my mother's car.'

Matty was thrilled. She was glad now she was wearing a really super and sophisticated dress. He probably thought she was about seventeen.

He hadn't driven her home. By Perth Water he slowed down and asked what time she was expected. 'I'm not,' she said with a shrug. 'My aunt doesn't care if I stay out all night.' Had it sounded like an invitation? Later, she had wondered if Patrick had taken it that way. At all events, he'd said, 'Why don't we go to my brother's flat? He won't be there—he lives up in the North-West and only comes down to Perth occasionally.'

Why not? Matty thought it a wonderful idea. The thought of going back to Peppertree Lodge wasn't an attractive one, and it was exhilarating—and flattering —to have someone like Patrick Dean pay her attention.

'How will we get in?' she asked a little later as they went up the stairs in the apartment block, her hand in his.

He looked at her and grinned.

'I managed to get hold of Dirk's key once and I had another one cut. I come here now and again when it suits me—I don't mess anything up, and he's never guessed.'

It was a beautiful flat. The front door opened straight into the big living room that was thickly carpeted, luxuriously furnished. There was a kitchenette, and off the living room a bedroom with a double bed and an en suite bathroom. Matty saw bath salts, body cologne, perfume in the bathroom, and asked Patrick curiously, 'Is your brother married?'

'No,' Patrick said, and added carelessly, 'He brings his girl-friends here. He thinks it's safer than asking them home and getting trapped. Marriage is anathema to him. He's supposed to be my half-brother, not my brother,' he tossed in rather mysteriously.

After that, Matty forgot about Dirk. The flat was fabulous to her after the austerity of Peppertree Lodge, and she took off her shoes to enjoy the feel of the thick carpet under her bare feet. Patrick put on the radiogram, but turned it well down so that the neighbours wouldn't hear it. He got drinks from the cocktail cabinet—something sweetish with gin in it for Matty, whisky and soda for himself.

'Won't your brother—your *half*-brother—notice if we drink his stuff?' she asked with a giggle.

'Oh, if we get through too much I'll buy some more and nip in and replace it,' Patrick said airily. They sat on the sofa his arm around her shoulders, drinking, and talking about themselves, and Matty thought it was exciting and romantic and just a little bit wicked. Every now and again Patrick refilled their glasses, and put his arm around her again, and soon everything became a little blurred. Matty knew she told him about the miseries of Peppertree Lodge, about Glenna Downs and the money that would be hers when she was twenty-one, and about the plans she and Maisie were making for a trip overseas as soon as she left school. Patrick too talked about himself. He told Matty about the stepfather who had legally adopted him, and wanted him to join the family accountancy firm later on. He didn't want to do that. He wanted to work on his half-brother's cattle station. Matty had vague memories of him looking broodingly into his glass and saying he'd let her into a secret. She was a little vague about what the secret was—something to do with his mother having run away before he was born, and his belief that half the cattle station should really be his. What they talked about after that, or what happened, she couldn't remember. She knew Patrick had kissed her quite a lot, and that she had been sick in the bathroom. And that she had felt cold. After that—nothing.

Aeons later she had pulled herself out of a river of sleep as thick and heavy as treacle, to discover where she was, and that it was early morning. All her feeling of romance and excitement had gone. She had felt frightened—too frightened even to cry, which was what she wanted to do.

What had happened? What had she done?

She had lain very still in the big bed, her mind, despite the headache that made her temples throb, exploring minutely every sensation in every part of her body. Nothing felt different. Nothing—hurt. Except her head.

She glanced warily at the dark-haired boy asleep so heavily on the other side of the bed. He must have drunk too much too. But they hadn't done anything, she was sure of it. Nothing except take their clothes off. How could you—do anything—when you were so drunk? she thought, sickened and ashamed.

She slithered out of the bed naked. Her clothes must be in the sitting room, and she knew what she was going to do. She was going to get dressed as fast as ever she could, and then she was going to call a taxi and disappear before Patrick even woke up. He'd never know she'd been there all night. She couldn't bear for him to know. Other girls slept around—even girls her own age—but not Matty Segal.

With hammering heart she tiptoed through to the other room. But before she'd even reached her dis-

carded clothes, there was a sharp click and the front
door opened. And Dirk Reasoner came in ...

Matty, lying in bed in the Fitzroys' house, heard herself utter a stifled gasp and turned on her side.
Couldn't she possibly have managed to get through the
rest of her life without meeting that man again?
Couldn't it at least have been put off until she was old
enough, mature enough, not to care?

But it doesn't matter, she told herself. Patrick would
have assured him that nothing had happened. Though
if he had, it didn't seem to have altered his opinion of
her. That much was clear from the way he'd looked at
her tonight.

CHAPTER THREE

SHE woke late the next morning, and then it was because Nerida Simmonds knocked on the door and came in.

'Are you awake, Matty?' she asked. She was a pretty, rather dreamy girl of seventeen or eighteen. 'Rona said to let you sleep, but my mother thought someone should wake you. All the men have gone out on the run, and we're going to have a game of tennis. Do you want to play?'

'I'd like to.' Matty sat up in bed and smiled at her. It was pleasant to find that Nerida was kindly disposed towards her, and it was a relief to know that Dirk Reasoner—and Lance—were both at least temporarily off the scene.

'There'll just be us four girls playing,' Nerida added. 'Shall I bring you some tea and toast or do you want me to ask Mary to cook you some steak and eggs?'

'Tea and toast will suit me, thank you.' Matty reached for her robe and Nerida pattered off. It was almost ten o'clock, Matty discovered—and Rona would have let her sleep till noon! She took a quick shower and came back to find her breakfast tray there. She poured a cup of tea, then left it to cool a little while she got into her white dress. It would be quite suitable for tennis, though it was ironic that her shorts, so out of place yesterday, would have been ideal today. When she found her way out to the tennis court, after taking her tray to the kitchen, she found the other three girls playing a game of cut-throat, and she sat on a seat under the trees and watched them. Nerida called a greeting and Helen waved her racquet, but Rona merely gave her an unsmiling nod.

All the same, possibly because it was too hot to play tennis consistently without a break, she was included in the morning's play, and proved herself able to hold her own. When, later, the Simmonds sisters had a game of singles, Rona went over to the house for cool drinks. Matty had suspected she might stay away long enough for the others to finish their set, but she didn't. She came back promptly with glasses and a big jug of squash, and for a few minutes she and Matty sat in silence, drinking the ice-cold fruit juice and watching the game. Matty had begun to feel a lot more cheerful, and she blinked with shock when Rona said abruptly,

'I suppose you're up this way hoping to find yourself a rich husband at the race meetings.'

Matty's lips parted in protest, but before she could speak the other girl continued swiftly, tossing back the blonde hair that was kept back from her face by a narrow white silk band, 'Don't start getting ideas about Dirk Reasoner, anyhow. He's not interested, and he's my property, in case you don't know.'

'Dirk Reasoner?' Matty exclaimed—not because he was Rona's property, but because it was ludicrous she should get ideas about *him*. 'I wouldn't——'

'Don't start protesting. I saw you last night while we were dancing—staring into his eyes and trying to work up something with him. It was the most obvious thing I've ever seen done.'

'I don't know what you mean,' said Matty, flushing. 'We were just talking.'

'About what?' Rona snapped, and Matty bit her lip.

'About—about horses. Nothing important.' She found it hard to be polite to Rona, and without really meaning to she asked her, 'Don't you honestly remember me at school, Rona?'

The blue eyes that met her own were deliberately

blank. 'No, I don't. As far as I'm concerned, you didn't go there.'

'Well, I remember you,' Matty said slowly. 'I remember once—at a concert—you played the piano. You played the Minute Waltz.'

'Oh, don't try that on,' Rona scoffed. 'I expect Lance told you I played the piano. Don't kid yourself *he's* ever likely to be serious about your kind of girl either, by the way. He's not.'

Matty felt a shiver of anger run over her nerves. She wasn't interested in Lance's intentions, but she didn't like Rona's tone. 'What do you mean—my kind of girl?'

Rona raised her eyebrows and looked amused. 'Well, you might not actually be a circus girl, but you still fit into that category. Traipsing round the provincial races with a bookmaker. Lance really shouldn't have invited you here. You may be too obtuse to have noticed it, but my parents are embarrassed.'

Matty twirled her glass around nervily in her hand and said bluntly, 'I'm not stupid, Rona. You've made very sure I know I'm not welcome, haven't you? I'm sorry if your parents are embarrassed, but I don't see why they should be. I haven't been impolite or made a nuisance of myself, and isn't Lance free to choose his own friends, the same as you are?'

'Well, of course—but *you* are *out*,' said Rona, and added vindictively, 'If you must know, no associate of Jerry Bridle's is welcome in this house. I'll tell you now so you'll understand—he cheated me last year over a bet—a big bet. He owed me a lot of money and he refused to pay it. None of us would ever lay a bet with him again.'

Matty's heart was pounding. She didn't believe a word of what Rona had said. Jerry just wasn't like that. Rona was lying, and she was on the verge of telling her so. The other girl watched her maliciously, ready, she supposed, for a rude outburst, and with an effort she controlled herself. She said mildly, knowing her eyes were angry, 'I think there must have been a misunderstanding. My uncle wouldn't cheat anyone—he's terribly honest.'

'Ha *ha*!' said Rona inelegantly, and kicked at a pebble with the toe of her tennis shoe. 'Anyhow, now you know exactly what we think of your lot, and why we don't want you here. So don't imagine Lance cares a cent about you, and lay *right* off Dirk. Do you understand?'

Matty didn't answer. The curious thought came into her head that she'd sooner spend a whole day in Dirk Reasoner's company than half an hour with Rona Fitzroy.

During that afternoon the rest of the guests arrived—four more girls, half a dozen young men, another middle-aged couple. There was a lot of laughter and excited talk and scurrying round as sleeping arrangements were made, and three tents were put up on the side lawn.

Matty, even though she knew herself an outsider, began to relax. The newcomers were friendly, though not terribly curious about her. They were more interested in catching up on each other's news and discussing what had been happening in their lives since last they met. One of the girls, Alice Derwent, actually remembered Matty from school.

When the men came back to the homestead, afternoon tea was served on the verandah—and beer for those who preferred it. In the general confusion of more greetings, more gossip, Matty was hardly noticed. Except by Dirk Reasoner who, for some motive she couldn't work out, came to stand near her and ask if she'd had a nice day.

'We played tennis,' she said non-committally.

'You're settling down, then. Not feeling so prickly.'

Matty touched her upper lip with her tongue nervously, and Rona called from along the verandah, 'Dirk, come and meet some of these people!'

Matty was on her own again and it was a good ten minutes before Lance bothered to come and speak to her.

'I hope you brought something to wear to the barbecue tonight,' he said after a moment, and his eyes went over her in a way that made her shrink into herself.

'Oh yes,' she said, and added wryly, 'Don't worry, I shan't make an exhibition of myself.'

'I didn't suggest you would,' he said. His glance strayed away to one of the other girls—to Alice Derwent, in fact—and a few seconds later he excused himself. 'I'm afraid I'll have to go and talk to Alice Derwent. I've been detailed to look after her—she's new up here.'

'Go ahead, don't mind me,' Matty said carelessly, well aware that she was being slighted—that Rona had probably engineered this. 'Alice is a nice girl,' she went on deliberately. 'I knew her at school.' Lance looked at her sharply, suspiciously, and she very nearly laughed. 'I did go to the same school as Rona,' she assured him. 'We certainly live in a democracy, don't we?—when a girl of my kind can go to the same school as the daughter of a—a cattle baron.'

Lance looked discomfited, but it didn't stop him from leaving her alone while he went back to Alice.

Tea over, the men went outside to fix up the barbecue—to set up lights and bring long trestle tables from the storage sheds. And the girls began a rush on the bathrooms. Matty was now sharing the white and yellow room with at least a couple of other girls, and when she made her way there, she found the room in some confusion—the wardrobe doors open, long dresses hanging up, an array of evening sandals and underskirts, combs and curlers and assorted garments scattered about. She'd seen some of the girls queueing laughingly outside the bathroom, and others waiting a turn in the shower room at the end of the side verandah. The second inside bathroom had been declared solely for the use of the older people.

Matty looked for her suitcase—and couldn't find it. And her long black and tan dress that she'd hung in the wardrobe after lunch—it simply wasn't there. Her peach-coloured dress had gone too. Nor were her pyjamas under the pillow on the bed she'd slept in last night.

More than a little disconcerted, she stepped on to the verandah where a couple of stretchers had been made up, but none of her things were there. Obviously someone had moved them—without telling her—and after a moment's thought she decided to look for Alice or Nerida and see what she could find out. For reasons she didn't go into, she preferred not to ask Rona. She wandered round the verandah in the direction of the shower room, and to her dismay found Rona there, leaning against the rails and smoking a cigarette. A tall older girl named Lesley had just come out of the shower room, and Alice went in as Matty turned the corner.

'I suppose you're looking for your clothes,' said Rona, her blue eyes cold and unfriendly.

'Yes,' Matty agreed, and didn't qualify it.

'They've been moved out. You can't expect a room to yourself when other people have been invited here weeks ago.'

'No, of course not,' Matty agreed, keeping her temper with difficulty.

'I've had your stuff moved to the little back verandah—along from the pantry and the flower room,' said Rona, blowing smoke so that it curled round Matty's face. 'There's a bed there—well out of the way,' she concluded with an unpleasant smile.

'Out of the way?' Matty echoed uncomprehendingly.

Rona raised her eyebrows. 'Isn't Lance sleeping with you tonight? Or who is it to be? I'm sure someone will oblige. It was pretty obvious what was going on last night when you disappeared so early and Lance excused himself not ten minutes later—oh!'

Matty's hand had flown up and before she'd known what she was doing she'd slapped the other girl's face—hard. Rona's mouth was wide open on an exclamation.

'Why, you vicious little cat! How *dare* you?' She dropped her cigarette on the floor and ground it under the heel of her slipper. She looked as if she were about to scratch Matty's eyes out, and Matty, appalled at what she had done, stood as though petrified for a moment. Then, just as Rona's hand came up, she turned and began to run.

She ran pantingly—not in search of the little back verandah where her clothes had been put, but down the steps and into the garden. Anywhere. Her face was white and when she stopped running it was to discover she was heading straight for the place where the barbecue was being set up. She about-faced at once and stood trembling, not knowing where to go, and wanting nothing so much as to escape from Bunda Bunda and all the people here. How dared Rona suggest she would let Lance make love to her—sleep with her? Was that what Mr and Mrs Fitzroy thought too? Was that what Dirk Reasoner thought? Oh yes, she reflected bitterly, Dirk Reasoner would believe that of her—with no difficulty whatsoever.

'What's the matter?'

Matty started guiltily. It was Dirk's voice and it was close behind her.

'Are you looking for Lance? He's——'

'No!' she exclaimed violently. 'I'm not looking for Lance. I—why should I be?'

'That would be obvious,' he said dryly, and she swung around and found herself staring straight into his dark eyes.

'You—*you* think he slept with me last night, don't you?' she breathed, her face white. 'Oh, how I hate you all! I can't imagine why my uncle thinks outback people are the best in the world—they——'

'Now stop it!' He had reached out a hand, and grasping her by the arm gave her a very untender shaking. 'Don't go trying to read my mind. We don't know each other all that well—yet ... All I meant was that as it was Lance who invited you here, who else in hell *would* you be looking for? All the girls are inside getting ready for the party—you're not looking for any of them ... Why aren't you queueing up for the shower too, anyhow?'

'Because I'm not interested in the party,' Matty said wildly. 'I want to go back to Kurranulla.' Without the least difficulty she could have burst into tears, and she wrenched her arm from Dirk's grasp and said furiously, 'Let me alone!'

'Hold on.' His voice was harsh and she hadn't escaped him after all, because now he had hold of her far more roughly, and with a movement that almost jerked her off her feet he made her captive between himself and the trunk of a gum tree. His hands pressed on her shoulders, so that she felt the unyielding tree-trunk hard against her shoulder blades. 'Is this tantrum you're throwing because Lance has been paying some attention to Alice whatever her name is? Or what's it all about?'

'It's nothing to do with you,' she said shakily. 'And I don't care who Lance pays attention to—or—or any of you,' she finished incoherently.

'All right, all right, if that's the way you feel,' he

said. But instead of him releasing her as she had expected him to, his eyes moved slowly to her mouth, then back to her eyes, and they stared at each other for a long moment. Suddenly, almost violently, his hands left her shoulders to rest firmly one at each side of her head. His body came hard against hers and he put his mouth to her lips and kissed her.

Matty couldn't move. With the tree at her back and his bulk pressing against her, there was not a thing she could do. Through the thin cotton of her dress she could feel his warmth—the hardness of his chest, the muscles of his abdomen. And soon she had the disturbing knowledge that he was sexually stirred.

When he lifted his mouth from hers and looked down into her face, his eyes dark, she stared back at him dumbly. Her heart was beating fast and she was confusedly aware of what was happening in his body. It seemed a lifetime before she managed to say huskily, 'What—what do you want?'

'I'll give you just three guesses,' he said, and then with a slow deliberation he drew away from her. 'But it's not the time or the place, is it? You'd better go back inside and get your shower before the men move in. No one's going to take you to Kurranulla tonight, so you'll have to make the best of things. It's the only intelligent course to take.'

Matty stood as if paralysed for perhaps five seconds, and then she ran. Even before she started running she was breathing fast. She found the little back verandah —she found a wall light and switched it on, though it wasn't anything like dark yet. Her pale yellow bath towels were on the bed and her suitcase was on the bed too, half open. Her clothes had been bundled into it any old how, and she caught a glimpse of her black and tan dress.

The moment she pulled it out she saw that it had been torn. Ripped. From the high neckline almost to the waist. It was unwearable, and she stared at it for several seconds before the penny dropped.

Rona had done that—probably before she had slapped her face. She stood for a long moment, on the point of tears, her face white with shock. And then, quite suddenly, she felt absolutely furious with Rona Fitzroy. She was the rudest, most spiteful girl she had ever come across, and she wasn't going to be beaten. If Rona meant to stop her from coming to the party, then she was going to lose out. She'd wear her peach-coloured dress. It wasn't fresh and it certainly wouldn't match the long gowns she'd seen the other girls hanging up in their rooms, but it was pretty and it suited her and it would do. It would have to.

Quickly she searched through the jumbled contents of her suitcase and right at the bottom she found her dress. And then she gasped aloud. It too had been ripped. But why? Matty didn't really have to look far for the answer. She knew.

It wasn't because she was Jerry Bridle's niece, and it wasn't anything to do with Lance. It was because Dirk Reasoner had appeared to take a little notice of her. If Rona had known—which she couldn't have—that Dirk had kissed her just now, what would she have done? Matty wondered.

Her cheeks were burning, but she'd already made up her mind what she was going to do. She'd wear her white jeans—one of her good shirts—the violet silk. *Boots*. Mascara, eye-shadow——

Even as the thoughts formed in her mind, she was gaspingly gathering her clothes together, and in a matter of minutes she was in the bathroom, ahead of the male rush. She showered quickly, got into her clothes, and made up her face at the bathroom mirror. Rona hadn't even been civil enough to give her a bedroom to dress in.

It was going to be a nightmare of a party ...

In a number of ways it was. All the girls looked so pretty and glamorous in their long dresses, Matty felt as much out of place as a prickly pear in a rose garden. A complete outsider and an obvious one.

Even before she encountered Rona's bright-eyed spiteful look, she was conscious of an aloofness—an unspoken admission among the girls that she didn't belong here. Mrs Fitzroy looked right through her and Matty supposed she was thinking, 'What else would one expect, from that kind of girl?'

The attitude of the men was different. They looked at her, but they didn't step out of line by fraternising. Lance, who'd been occupied with Alice, came over to her and drawled out, 'Didn't you say you had a dress?'

'Yes,' Matty snapped, her eyes flashing. 'But I decided not to wear it. I thought it might be more in character if I wore this sort of thing.' She was being rude and she knew it, but hadn't Rona been rude? And wasn't Lance rude too, dropping her, to tag around with Alice Derwent on his sister's—or his mother's—orders? Anyhow, Matty no longer cared what anyone thought of her. She'd reached the unalterable conclusion that she hated outback people. In future she'd stick to Jerry, and not even to please him would she go within cooee of another homestead. The best people in the world! That was a laugh!

She got through the barbecue somehow, picked at a steak, ate some salad, drank two glasses of red wine. It was a buffet meal, very informal, and with everyone milling around it was hardly noticeable if she was alone and helping herself. Nevertheless, it irked her that Lance didn't even have the decency to look after her a little.

Strangely enough, Dirk came to ask her if she'd like a helping from any of the dishes of delectable-looking desserts that had been carried out to the tables by

Mary and two aboriginal girls, after the savoury dishes and the steaks had been demolished. He spoke to her with a polite smile, and it seemed unreal that he had made that pass at her earlier on in the garden. Matty smiled back stiffly and shook her head.

'No, thank you. I've finished eating.'

He gave her a sharp look and seemed on the point of saying something further, but changed his mind and moved away.

Later, when dancing began on the verandah, there was a general move indoors, but Matty stayed outside on the fringe of the area lit by the strings of coloured lights. No one was likely to ask her to dance—and not only because she was wearing boots. She stood and watched the comings and goings on the verandah, the dancers who dropped out for a cool drink or a breath of air. She saw Dirk dance with Rona, with Helen, with the tall girl called Lesley—and then with Rona again. She wondered *why* she watched him. He was different from the others—older, more mature, his build more powerful. In fact, he was a very positive, very aggressive personality.

Hands off Dirk Reasoner, Rona had said. And the thought came suddenly into Matty's head that if she could get hold of him, then she was going to monopolise him. Just to show Rona Fitzroy that she couldn't have it all her own way. She wasn't a saint that she could meekly take all that was handed out to her and not retaliate.

Her chance came not much later when she saw Dirk come down the steps and into the garden alone. Deliberately she started walking in his direction, and they met on the pathway under the bauhinias.

'It's Matty!' he exclaimed. 'Where have you been hiding yourself? I was coming to look for you. Would you like a drink?'

She shook her head, unable, now the time had come,

to do anything that was guaranteed to detain him.

'Perhaps you'd like to dance, then.' He put a hand on her wrist and her arm tingled curiously, but she made a small grimace and extended one back-booted foot.

'In these?'

'Why did you wear boots, for God's sake? I'm beginning to think you're some kind of an exhibitionist —or perhaps you have a kinky streak of masochism in your make-up … That's surely not the only kind of clothing you brought with you.'

'Oh, I brought a long dress,' she agreed. 'Black and tan silk, with sandals to match. Really pretty.'

'Yet you preferred to be—different.' His eyes skimmed over her bosom, its outline suggested by the fine silk of her violet shirt, lingered on her small waist, her flat tummy, then came back to her face and her shining hair. 'Fetching though you look, isn't it more polite to be orthodox?'

'I don't think I'm expected to know much about being polite or orthodox.' They had begun to stroll slowly along the path together, and the leaves of the bauhinias made shadows across Dirk's face so that he looked enigmatic. It was a hot night and he, like all the other males, had removed his coat. His dark face was in striking contrast to the white of his shirt, and again Matty was strongly aware of the dominating quality of his personality, and of the fact that he was somehow vastly different from every other man here. He was looking down at her questioningly, and she said, her voice low, 'Anyhow, I—I had no choice. I couldn't wear my dress. It was torn.' She flushed as she said it, suddenly aware of how it would sound after what he had seen last night.

His eyebrows drew together. 'Surely not Lance again?' he said dryly.

She ignored that. 'I didn't even put it on. It might

have been an accident, but—I'm not wanted here, you know. You said last night I wasn't expected, but I'm not wanted either. Anyone who can't see that must be blind,' she babbled on. 'It's not just that I wear the wrong clothes—I have the wrong kind of relations, too. I've been told that my uncle is a cheat. *I* don't believe it, but it seems everyone else here must. Something that happened last year over a bet Rona made at the races——'

They had paused and Dirk lit a cigarette—a tailor-made this time—and the flame of the lighter illuminated his features flickeringly so that Matty was fleetingly aware of the slightly—and somehow fascinatingly—crooked line of his nose. He flicked off his lighter and said brusquely, 'There was a dispute over what Jerry Bridle owed Rona for a win. I don't know any of the details, and I don't want to, but I do know that the stewards came down in your uncle's favour.'

Matty's heart raced. So there! Jerry was right! She had known it! She said scornfully, 'But you—and everyone—thought they were wrong. You must be rotten sports. I know my uncle wouldn't cheat—he's absolutely honest. He's looked after my affairs since I was twelve years old. It's—it's the Fitzroys who are the cheats——'

'There you go again,' he said coolly. 'You haven't a clue what I think and I certainly didn't say I thought the stewards were wrong, so don't get excited and act as if you've got a persecution complex.'

Matty bit her lip and felt somewhat cut down to size. He was standing so close to her she could feel his body warmth as she watched him draw on his cigarette, then turn aside to exhale. The faint sound of music drifted across the garden towards them as he told her, 'As far as I'm concerned, the incident is over and forgotten, and I'm not nominating cheats on either side.'

There was a little silence and suddenly she needed a cigarette, and she put out her hand in a vague gesture. Dirk put the cigarette he had started smoking between her fingers, and while she drew on it deeply and steadyingly, he lit another one for himself. Then disconcertingly he came back to the subject of her dress.

'So what was this accident that happened to your dress? How did it get torn?'

She shrugged. 'I don't know. It must have happened when all my things were moved. My morals are under suspicion, you know.'

'What the hell are you gabbing about?' he asked roughly, and oddly, it sounded as if he had known her for years. 'What's been happening now? Why were your things moved?'

'Well, you saw Lance—mauling me last night, didn't you? And I suppose you heard that he——' She stopped and swallowed, then went on flatly, 'He was supposed to have followed me to bed later? As a result, I've been given a very special secluded corner of my own. All my belongings have been shifted to the little back verandah near the flower room—and the pantry— if you're interested. I'm supposed to be trying to work up something with you too, you know.' She stopped with the sudden feeling that she'd gone too far, and glancing at him through her lashes, she saw that he was looking at the tip of his cigarette and that his wide mouth was set in a grim line. Then unexpectedly he flung his cigarette on the ground, set his foot on it and swung round to take her by the shoulders.

'And *are* you?' he asked sharply.

'Am I—am I—what?' she stammered. Fires raced up her arm and she had begun to tremble. Compulsively her mind had pivoted back to his earlier embrace, when he had laid his body against hers, his lips on hers, and now she could feel her own body responding disturbingly to the passion that had risen in him then. 'I don't know what you mean,' she whispered nervily.

His fingers moved against the warm silk of her shirt and she felt the movement like a caress on her skin.

'*Are* you trying to work up something with me?' His voice was low but distinct.

She tried to laugh. 'How would you get that idea?'

'Perhaps I'm extra sensitive to your vibrations.' He pulled her to him as he spoke, then used one hand to grip her by the hair at the back of her neck and force her head up. With his other hand he freed her shirt from her waistband, then slid it up and under her flimsy bra to her breast. She felt her nipple contract and a shiver run through her, and his mouth came down to hers. She closed her eyes and several drowning seconds passed while she was aware of nothing but the fact that she was balanced on the edge of a painful pleasure. It was only her cigarette burning her fingers that brought her back to a sense of reality.

Dirk raised his head a little.

'What's the matter? Why did you withdraw like that?'

'I—my cigarette burned me,' she breathed, ashamed and bewildered now. She pulled away a little and put her stinging fingers to her mouth and sucked them. The thought came into her mind that she was certainly having a revenge on Rona—though Rona would never know about it. Her breathing fast, she began to stuff her shirt back into her pants.

He watched her and then asked, 'Am I mistaken, or was that an invitation you gave me a moment ago?'

'I—how could I have stopped you?' Her cheeks were crimson.

'If you'd really wanted to you could have,' he said, sounding vaguely amused. 'But I didn't mean letting me stroke your nipple, if that's what you're talking about. I meant what you said earlier—about the back verandah.'

Mortified, she choked out, 'Of course it wasn't an invitation!'

'It could have been,' he said dryly. 'And *did* Lance follow you to your bed last night?'

'No,' she gasped out. 'What—what do you think I am?'

He smiled crookedly in the darkness. 'I'm not quite sure what you are yet: I'm still in the process of finding out. It's a long time since we last met, don't forget ... I do get the idea it wouldn't be very hard to seduce you, but I'm beginning to doubt whether you've packed very much—sophisticated experience into the last four years of your life. Has there been anyone much since Patrick?'

Matty didn't answer what was, when she thought about it, a decidedly double-barrelled question, because at that moment they were interrupted by a voice —Rona's, of course—calling Dirk.

'That's it,' he remarked. 'I've long grown out of coming when I'm called, but if we don't move then we're going to be looked for. Have you finished putting yourself back together again?'

Matty nodded but didn't speak. Rona was going to know she had been monopolising her property, and though she had wanted just that not very long ago, now it gave her little satisfaction. In fact she was beginning to wish she hadn't taken that first step in Dirk's direction when she saw him come into the garden. She'd be a whole lot safer keeping right away from him.

When they reached the coloured lights, she drifted away from him, and he let her go. She would have liked to disappear completely—something that seemed to be becoming a habit—but she didn't fancy going to bed on the verandah just yet. For how much longer would the party continue? she wondered.

It continued till dawn, she was to discover.

And most of that time she spent sitting safely on the verandah, not too close to the lights, not too conspicuous, listening to the music, hearing snatches of conversation, and trying not to think. Surely, she thought wryly, when at last she made her way to bed to find the light of dawn already touching the edge of the world—surely no one would bother her now, if she had had any fears that she might have been bothered.

She had stopped worrying exactly what Dirk had meant when he'd asked had there been anyone since Patrick. He couldn't possibly believe that she and Patrick had made love.

But that was wrong. She knew he could—and probably did.

CHAPTER FOUR

NEARLY everyone slept half the next day through, but Matty was wakened early by sounds from the kitchen, and got up and showered and dressed—in black jeans, a red and white checked shirt. She had tea and toast in the breakfast room, feeling rather limp and depressed, and someone came in while she was pouring her second cup of tea. It was Dirk, and she coloured furiously at the sight of him.

'Well, how did you sleep in your place of exile?'

'Oh, I slept,' she said non-committally.

'I thought you might be up.' He sat down opposite her and reached for the teapot. 'We seem to be the last survivors, don't we? What are your plans?'

'To get back to Kurranulla the minute I can,' she said flatly.

'You're not enjoying yourself?' His eyes mocked her, and she shook her head and looked away from him, remembering last night.

'I'm going to ask Don Graham to drive me into town this morning.'

'You'll have missed him—he'll be out on the run. Anyhow, there's no need to ask anyone to put themselves out for you. If you wait till this afternoon you can come with me.'

Matty's heart lurched. She didn't know that she wanted to go with him—be indebted to him. But on the other hand, why not think of it as making use of him? Rona of course would be livid . . .

'Thank you,' she said coolly. 'I'll do that.'

She finished drinking her tea and left the table.

She didn't know how Dirk put in what was left of

the morning. Matty went to see Marie Graham. True enough, Don was out, and the boys had gone with him, but Marie was home, baking. Matty sat on the kitchen stool and watched her and fenced all her questions about the house party.

'They're all sleeping it off this morning,' she said lightly as Marie put a tray of scones in the oven. 'I'm sorry you and Don weren't there last night.'

'Oh well, we come under the heading of employees with the Fitzroys,' Marie shrugged. 'I don't mind it being that way. We have our own friends and enjoy our own get-togethers. Don and I don't play bridge, and we're a bit old to mix with Rona's and Lance's friends. How did you get on with Lance, by the way?—not that I want to pry.'

'Oh, all right,' said Matty, then added flippantly, 'But I shan't cry when we say goodbye. I'm leaving this afternoon, as a matter of fact, so will you please say goodbye to Don and the boys for me?' She didn't tell Marie who was driving her to town, and she didn't air her grievances about the Fitzroys and their methods of entertaining either. That was all very nearly over and done with, thank goodness.

Lunch was late, and it was a cold buffet meal, served on the wide verandah. There was chicken and turkey and ham, loads of salads and fruits, and everyone was full of fun and chatter. Matty in jeans and shirt now looked no different from anyone else, but by now she couldn't have joined in and felt one of them to save her life. From snatches of talk, she discovered they were planning a moonlight picnic that night—'Something really ethnic,' she heard one of the girls from Perth say. 'Lance says we'll have a great roaring fire and cook our steaks on the blade of a shovel. Billy tea, *of course*——' 'And skinny-dipping in the river afterwards,' one of the boys put in, and glanced laughingly across at Matty as he said it.

Matty smiled back at him. It could—under other circumstances—have been a lot of fun, it really could. Not that she'd have been prepared to go skinny-dipping —unless, perhaps, they were all doing it.

Rona didn't address a single word to Matty, who had discovered the meaning of the old cliché, If looks could kill. If they could, she'd certainly have dropped dead the moment Rona set eyes on her. During lunch, Lance left Alice's side to stroll across to Matty and ask her coldly, 'How are you today? Got over your pique or whatever it was about?'

'Yes, thank you,' she said brightly after an instant of shock.

'Good. But don't go and wear a long dress for the picnic tonight, will you?'

'If I were coming to the picnic, I just might,' she retorted. 'But I'm leaving this afternoon, Lance. With Dirk Reasoner,' she concluded, knowing she'd have to tell him some time.

'What? You—you can't do that,' he stuttered. 'Not when I asked you here. You can't just go off with some-one else like that!' His glance strayed in his sister's direction. 'Not with Dirk, of all people. Rona will be —she'll be *ropeable*!'

'I'm sorry, Lance, I can't help that,' said Matty. 'You know it's best for me to go really. You shouldn't have asked me here in the first place, should you?'

'If you'd behaved decently it would have been all right,' he said belligerently. 'Rona would have sim-mered down—the parents would have been philoso-phical. But you had to go and make eyes at Dirk. That's why you had to be taught a lesson.'

'I've certainly learnt it,' Matty said dryly. What was the use of trying to be rational? She was in the wrong —it was all her fault—that was Lance's attitude. She turned away, but he grabbed her by the arm and said in her ear, 'You're not to do this, do you hear?'

'Argue it out with Dirk,' Matty said wearily, and after a second he let her go.

When Dirk joined her a few minutes later she said without preamble, 'I've just been told I'm not to go with you.'

His mouth twisted cynically. 'Well, it's up to you. I don't know what you've been hoping to accomplish here.'

'I haven't been hoping to accomplish anything,' she said hotly. 'All I want is to go back to my uncle.'

'Then be ready as early as you like after lunch,' he said briskly.

Matty had finished lunch. So she packed her suitcase, and then went to find her host and hostess and thank them for having her. She didn't tell them who was taking her in to Kurranulla and they weren't sufficiently interested to enquire, but she supposed they'd find out later on. The little ceremony over, she went and fetched her suitcase.

Out on the driveway, she found Dirk talking to Lance, who turned to her unsmilingly as she appeared.

'Well, goodbye,' he said. 'I suppose if you must go you must. I won't stay and wave goodbye—we're getting things organised for the picnic tonight. I daresay I'll see you at the races tomorrow.'

'Yes. I'll be with my uncle,' Matty said levelly. 'Thank you for inviting me here, Lance. Goodbye.'

A couple of minutes later she and Dirk were on their way.

'You might like to know I apologised to Lance for taking you away,' he told her as they drove off. 'I explained that you were worried about your uncle. He's a sick man, isn't he?'

Matty glanced at him quickly and saw that he was looking serious. 'He's all right now,' she said. 'He had a slight heart attack a few weeks ago, but he took a rest and he's okay.'

'Is that what he says? You're fond of him, aren't you?'

'Yes. He's looked after me for a long time.'

'Has he?' Dirk sounded sceptical. 'Well, all I can say is you could have been more strictly supervised a few years ago.'

Matty flushed and stared out at the countryside. 'He had to be away most of the time at the provincial race meetings,' she said stiffly. 'But he looked after my schooling and—well, everything. He looked after my—my affairs for me too.'

'Your affairs?'

'My money—my *business* affairs,' she said with annoyance, and added explosively, 'You have a very low opinion of me, haven't you. All because of that—that night. That's why you—kissed me the way you did yesterday, too, isn't it?'

He turned his head and gave her a cool glance. 'No, it's not why, as a matter of fact. The simple fact is, you're not fifteen now,' he finished laconically. 'So you can expect to be kissed that way.'

Matty swallowed. A couple of days ago she would never have believed she could be sitting beside him in his car talking to him like this. But she hadn't only lived through meeting him again—she'd also come out the other side, and now she didn't know what she felt about him. She asked with a touch of desperation, 'Where's Patrick these days?'

'At this moment, I'm not altogether sure where he is. In Perth, quite possibly. He flew down to collect his girl-friend and bring her back for race week, but as they haven't turned up yet, I'm beginning to think Lyndal may have other ideas as to how she wants to be entertained. She's not a country girl.'

'Are she and Patrick engaged?' Matty asked cautiously. She didn't want to appear over-interested, but it seemed a safe enough subject.

'I suppose you could call it that,' said Dirk. 'They've been sleeping together for some time, and both the Deans and the Stevens are hoping they'll make it legal, young though they are.'

'Oh. Is he working in Perth? He used to say he wanted to work here.'

Dirk frowned. 'He started doing an accountancy course, but he dropped out of that and went off to Indonesia. He's been jackerooing for me for the past few months, but only on a trial basis. In my opinion, he'd be better off in his father's firm.'

'His stepfather's firm, you mean,' she corrected him. 'Don't you want him here?'

'No, I don't.'

'Why not?' she asked aggressively, and he told her briefly, 'That's my business. You're not still interested, I hope. I told you he has a girl-friend.'

'But they're not engaged,' she said perversely. She wondered if he thought she wasn't good enough for Patrick. 'And if I were interested, it wouldn't be anything to do with you. You might have told him he wasn't to see me any more while we were still at school, but we're both grown up now.'

'I'm well aware of that,' he agreed dryly. 'I'd say you've definitely reached a marriageable age.' His eyes flicked over her and back to the track they were following. 'How old are you? Twenty?'

'Nearly,' she said frigidly. 'But I'm not interested in marriage.'

He cast her a mocking look. 'Exactly how does one take a remark like that, I wonder?'

'You can take it however you like. I don't care,' she snapped, her cheeks burning.

They talked very little after that, and when they reached the hotel in town he carried her suitcase in for her, said goodbye, and added that he was going on to Moonak. Matty breathed a sigh of relief at the news and went to find her uncle.

Jerry was not about, however, and she didn't see him until dinner time. And then he told her something that was to change her whole life.

Their conversation began over dinner when he wanted to know how she had enjoyed her stay at Bunda Bunda, and expressed surprise that she was back in town already.

'Did you have a good time, Treasure—meet some nice people?—some nice fellows?'

Matty wrinkled her nose. 'Oh, it was all right. But I'm glad to be back with you, Jerry. The Fitzroys are snobs and Lance——' She stopped and her grimace deepened.

'You didn't go much on him?' he asked, looking at her rather anxiously. Matty looked back at him and the remark Dirk had made came back into her mind—— He's a sick man. His face did look strained, lined. Yet he could be no more than fifty-two or three. Instead of answering him she put a hand impulsively on his wrist 'Jerry, how are you feeling? You look tired.'

'Now don't tell me that, Matty,' he said with a wry grin. 'I'm fine. It's you I want to talk about, anyhow, not me. Who brought you back to town, by the way? Was it young Fitzroy?'

'No. It was Mr Reasoner,' Matty told him. She used the formal address deliberately, but she flushed all the same, and turned her head aside hoping her uncle wouldn't notice her heightened colour.

His eyes brightened with interest. 'Now that's a man I like. Jim said he was sure to be at Bunda Bunda. I'm glad you met him ... If you didn't fancy Lance, then what about Dirk. You must have made a hit with him since he drove you in. Did he ask you out to Moonak?'

Matty ate another mouthful of her roast beef before she answered him.

'I didn't make a hit with anyone, Jerry,' she said firmly, 'and if you're trying to find a husband for me I wish you'd forget it. And don't try to pack me off to any more house parties either, I'd rather stay with you.'

Jerry sighed and there was a rather long silence. Then he said heavily, 'Matty, it's important to me you should meet people—think about getting married. I lied to you just now when I said I was fine. I'm a sick man. This is the last time I'll come up for the Kurranulla Round, or for any other round. I saw two specialists in Perth. Both of them told me to pull my horns in—to quit work, in fact. And both of them gave me—well, no more than a few months to live.' He hadn't finished his dinner and now he fiddled awkwardly with his knife, and didn't look at Matty. She felt her heart contract with fear, and she stared at him helplessly. Dirk had been right, it seemed—terribly right.

'Oh, Jerry!' she exclaimed, anguished. 'And you're worried about getting me married—when you shouldn't even have come up here!' She leaned towards him, her grey-green eyes dark with concern. 'You *must* give up work. We can use my money—I have plenty for the two of us. The doctors may be wrong —if you rest——'

He stopped her with a gesture. 'No, Treasure. It's no use, and I'm not going to fool myself. And there's something else I've got to tell you about.' He pushed his chair back. 'Come upstairs to my room.'

She hadn't the faintest idea what he was going to tell her as she went up the stairs with him, but when they reached his room and the door was closed and they were both sitting down, he told her bluntly, 'You don't have any money, Matty.'

She stared at him uncomprehendingly. 'But the—the

investments my mother made,' she stammered.

He stared down at his square brown hands, and she saw his mouth work. Then he raised his head and looked at her. 'Your mother meant well when she left me in charge of your money, Matty. But—did you know I used to be a gambler?'

'I—I know you used to follow the races in Queensland, that you used to bet. But I thought——'

'You thought I'd given it up. And so did Grace. But she shouldn't have trusted me. Once a gambler, always a gambler.' He spread his hands hopelessly. 'I guess Grace thought Maisie would keep me on an even keel, but my wife never even knew what I was doing. I'm not asking you to understand—you've never been mixed up with a compulsive gambler and I hope to God you never will be.' He broke off and laughed bitterly, brokenly. 'Listen to me talking! Of course you've been mixed up with a gambler—I've lost all your money for you—every cent of it.'

'But how?' Matty couldn't take it in. There had been—there must have been—such a lot of money.

'How? Not long after your mother died, I re-invested some of it—well, most of it—in a mining company that was being floated. I thought I'd make a mint. Instead, it went broke. So I bought into racehorses. I thought I'd make amends that way. For a while things went well, but my luck didn't hold—it wasn't good enough. There was your education, you see—and making sure you had everything your mother would have wished. Maisie always insisted you should have the best—and so you should. I've done average well as a bookmaker, but I've hit the bottom, lately. I've been —worried.'

He looked down at his hands again and Matty bit her lip. He looked so—so abject that her heart was wrung, and when he raised his eyes they were so full of shame it hurt to look back at him.

'You must despise me now—and it's too late for regrets. I'm finished. There's nothing more I can do. It's no use telling you I'm sorry, but believe me, I am.'

Stunned though she was by what he had told her, and still unable to take it in fully, Matty was more concerned about her uncle than she was about herself. He looked so ill, so utterly defeated, and she left her chair to go and kneel by him and put her hand over his. 'I don't despise you, Jerry. I—I understand how it must have happened. You meant well—and you've given me my education. I've had everything a girl could want. You mustn't worry about me, I'll be all right.'

He shook his head. 'Not if you're left to the mercy of that shrew Louise. She'll play on your good nature and make a slave of you the same as she did with Maisie. No—I wouldn't die happy if I left you with her. That's why I brought you up here—that's why I'm determined to see you married.'

Matty's face was pale.

'But I don't have to stay with Louise, Jerry. I can get work.'

'What kind of work?' he asked, and she saw the self-contempt in his eyes. 'You've had no training for anything. I won't have you going off to a jam factory every day and finishing up with a mate from the wrong side of the paddock fence. I've done enough damage to your life already. The very least I can do is see you get yourself a good husband, before I go to meet my Maker. If you don't care for Lance Fitzroy, there's Dirk Reasoner—there's his young brother—there are half a dozen decent, well-off fellows I can introduce you to up this way.'

Matty swallowed a sob that was half a laugh. This was crazy and it was sad. As if she could find someone to—to love and to marry, just like that——

'Please, Jerry,' she begged, 'stop it! I don't want to get married—I don't want to meet any men.'

'Oh, my God,' Jerry groaned, and his face looked greyer than it had before. 'I've done the hell of a thing to you, haven't I? But for my sake, won't you give it a fly?' He put a hand to his heart and for one ghastly moment Matty thought he was going to have an attack of some sort. She knew she simply couldn't go on upsetting him, and to humour him she told him shakily, 'All right, Jerry, I'll—I'll give it a fly, then. I'll—you can introduce me to—to some of these men. And if——' she stopped.

'If what?' he said eagerly, and already a little colour had come back into his face.

'Well, if we fell in love—— I couldn't marry anyone without that.'

'Well, of course not!' He actually smiled at her, his familiar slightly crooked smile. 'But it's not all that hard to fall in love, Matty. It only seems like there's something magic about love. We're all no more than human, and I'll guarantee no one would have much trouble falling in love with you. You're pretty and intelligent, and I'll lay you a hundred to one if you set your mind to it we'll have found someone you'll be happy to spend the rest of your life with before race week is over in Wanganup. You're a country girl born and bred—you'll be a winner in this part of the West.'

Matty smiled tremulously, unable to share his confidence.

'If you're invited to Moonak you'll accept?'

'Yes, of course,' she agreed. If Jerry only knew it, she had Buckley's chance of being invited *there*—and there was not a hope in the world that Dirk Reasoner would fall in love with her. As for her falling in love with him—it simply couldn't happen. But the thing was to go along with Jerry, to keep him happy. And certainly he was looking a lot more cheerful already.

'I'm glad that's over,' he said presently. 'It's been on my conscience—and now I have your co-operation . . .

Just one other thing, though—there's no need to tell anyone you've got nothing.'

'No, of course not, Jerry,' she agreed wryly.

She did a little thinking that night before she went to bed, and she shed a few tears over Jerry. She was going to have to give the impression of a girl ready and willing to fall in love. She thought fleetingly of the boys she'd met at Bunda Bunda. Nice people probably, all of them, but she'd started with a handicap. She'd have to begin all over again with someone new. But how on earth did one go about leading a man on to propose marriage? Wouldn't most men run if they knew a girl had that in mind, the moment she met them? In an odd sort of way, it would have been a relief to be invited to Moonak, she caught herself thinking. At least she knew Dirk Reasoner already—at least she wouldn't be starting cold. But what on earth was she dreaming about? She must be half asleep. It would be like trying to empty the sea with a teaspoon to set herself the task of snaring *him* . . .

Next morning Jerry was looking much more like himself, and Matty wished she could find that everything that had happened had been no more than a bad dream. But unfortunately it was all too true.

He told her at mid-morning that he'd drawn a horse for her in the Calcutta at the hotel. Miss Fitz, from the Fitzroys' stable.

'If it comes in first you'll win five hundred dollars, Treasure,' he told her, looking as pleased with himself as if he were offering her a fortune. Matty bit her lip. She was seeing him with new eyes now, and it was disturbing to discover him so different—so much weaker—than the man she had thought she knew. She'd never for an instant dreamed he'd have been anything but scrupulously honest and careful with her inheritance—and Maisie hadn't either, she reflected. It had been Maisie who always insisted she should have good clothes, the best of everything and no expense spared, and she remembered once hearing her aunt tell Jerry he should buy a home of his own, get Matty out of Peppertree Lodge.

Well, it was futile to go over the past.

For the races, Matty wore a sleeveless blue-green dress. It buttoned down the front from a high mandarin collar, but somehow was elegant rather than demure. Her freckles had been emphasised a little already by the sun, and she was careful to smooth on sunproof cream and to wear sunglasses. No use trying to attract men if your nose was red and peeling, she told herself with a rather cynical humour. She knew she was likely to see the people who'd been at Bunda Bunda today, and it was certain that Dirk Reasoner would be there. Her throat contracted nervously at the thought.

Once at the racecourse, she stayed in Jerry's vicinity except when she went to the rails to watch a race.

'Don't wander too far, Matty,' he'd told her. 'I want you nearby in case someone turns up I think you should meet.'

Matty met dozens of people. She also renewed her slight acquaintance with some of the Bunda Bunda crowd. Most of the girls smiled at her after they'd done a double take and finally realised who she was, and some of the boys asked if she was going on to Ridge Creek. But she got no invitations.

Lance kept clear of her. He was still escorting Alice Derwent around. She saw Dirk, though he only smiled at her from a distance. He was with Rona and Lesley, and Stuart Simmonds, and Matty tried to keep her eyes off him, hiding behind her sunglasses and wondering why the mere sight of him put her into a mild panic, so that her heart began to thump. Rona had turned her back on her, but that didn't worry Matty.

Miss Fitz came in first, and Jerry gave her her five hundred dollars. 'Take it now, Treasure—I'll be collecting it at the hotel later on your behalf. Have a bet —but not with me! You might double your money if you're lucky. I'll give you a tip for the next race.'

Matty listened, but she wasn't going to make a bet. For the first time, she was going to have to watch her pennies. 'Matilda Segal will never have to work— she'll have all the money in the world to spend as she likes.' So Louise had frequently remarked. But now Matty had nothing except the five hundred dollars in her handbag—and she was going to hang on to it.

'Matty Segal!'

The sound of her own name roused her from her rather sad thoughts and, startled, she looked up into the face of Patrick Dean, colour flooding her face.

'Good God!' Patrick was exclaiming, gripping her hands. 'Fancy running into you in this part of the world! Could anything be nicer?'

As she said a rather shaky, 'Hello,' he deftly removed her sunglasses, and his dark grey eyes went over her face exploringly. He hadn't changed greatly, she thought. In light blue denim pants and short-sleeved matching jacket, he was very good-looking, and there was still that touch of moodiness in his face that had fascinated her years ago. Yet he seemed strangely immature, and she realised she was comparing him with Dirk, and asked hurriedly, as if to hide her thoughts from herself, 'Where's your girl-friend?'

His face seemed to close up. 'Have you been talking to my brother? I don't have a girl-friend any more. Lyndal and I have split up and that's that ... Who are you here with, anyhow?' he continued, smiling again. 'Anyone who's likely to flatten me with a sledge-hammer if I carry you off to watch the next race?'

'No. I'm with my uncle, Jerry Bridle,' Matty told him. 'He's a bookmaker.' She'd grown used to saying that by now, and she waited for his reaction but he merely said cheerfully, 'Well—imagine that! It doesn't look as though you can present me just now—there's such a mob around him.'

He took Matty's arm possessively and they headed for the rails. The horses were still lining up for the start, but Patrick didn't seem terribly interested in them. He asked, his arm around her shoulders, 'Do you remember that night in Dirk's apartment? My God, didn't we get stinking drunk—too drunk to know what we were doing!'

He squeezed her shoulder slightly as he spoke, and chilling with shame but trying to treat it as lightly as he did, she said, 'We didn't do anything.'

'No? ... You were a terrific girl—game for anything. I've never forgotten you. I hope you haven't changed.'

Matty bit her lip and moved a little away from him. She hadn't been game for anything and she wasn't now, but she knew she had behaved in a way that invited trouble.

'Did you have that trip to Europe after you left school?' Patrick wanted to know.

'No, my aunt was ill so we didn't go.'

'Rotten luck!' he sympathised. 'How long before you turn twenty-one and come into that inheritance of yours?'

Yesterday that question wouldn't have bothered her, now she wished she'd never mentioned her prospects to Patrick. She could hardly tell him that her uncle had lost all her money for her, and she said evasively, 'I don't know that I'd exactly call it an inheritance. At any rate, I'm not even twenty yet.'

'All that young! So what are you doing with yourself—apart from popping up here at Kurranulla?'

'I've been helping my aunt in her guest-house,' she said briefly. Oddly, she felt even more edgy with him than she did with Dirk, perhaps because he was so—

flippant about that night in Perth. What was Lyndal like? she wondered inconsequentially. But they had split up, and now it seemed Patrick was all set to pay plenty of attention to Matty Segal. It occurred to her suddenly that here was someone she could—lead on —for her uncle's benefit. Instant attraction, but based on an earlier acquaintance. It could be made to sound quite convincing. But the idea didn't really appeal. Patrick might very well invite her to Moonak—but if he did, would he expect her to sleep with him? The thought brought her to her senses with a jolt.

'What have you been doing?' she asked, before he could put any more questions to her.

'Oh, I started accountancy, but I bombed out and Lyndal and I went off to Indonesia. Since then I've been jackerooing at Moonak, but nobody's happy about that except me. Dirk's always trying to shove me back to Perth and into accountancy—mainly because Lyndal isn't a country girl, as far as I can see. Well, he won't have that excuse to use next time he decides to give me an ear-bashing.'

The race began and they watched it, and then Patrick took her to the bar, where she had a lemonade and he had a couple of cans of beer, and presently she took him to meet Jerry.

'We're old friends from schooldays,' Patrick told Jerry promptly, and her uncle looked ultra-pleased. Matty could practically see his mind ticking over, and knew he was hoping already that something might come of this friendship. If Jerry were to suspect what she suspected—that if she were invited to Moonak Patrick would try to seduce her—he mightn't look quite so pleased.

She went to the barbecue that night with Patrick, out at the racecourse, and Jerry came with them. As Patrick turned the Hereford beef steaks they had bought, Jerry remarked,

'By the way, I couldn't get a room for Matty at the Ridge Creek Hotel. It slipped my mind to reserve it earlier. Any suggestions, Patrick?' Behind Patrick's back he sent Matty a conspiratorial wink, and she burned with shame. But worse still, she discovered Dirk had emerged from the crowd around the barbecue grill and had plainly heard what her uncle had said and had probably seen that wink. Oh God, she prayed, don't let Patrick fall for it. And she turned with a bright smile to Dirk and said with a casualness that was incredible, 'Oh, hello, Dirk. You know my uncle, I believe.'

'Sure I do. How goes it, Jerry?' Then as Patrick turned round and was for sure going to suggest Matty should come to Moonak, he continued, 'How would it suit you if I took Matty back to Moonak with me tonight? Would that meet with your approval?'

'You're too generous,' said Jerry. 'I gather you heard what I said just now. But I wasn't fishing for an invitation, believe me. I just thought you might know of someone in town who had a room to spare ... What do you think, Matty? Would you like that?'

'Of course she would,' Patrick put in. 'I was going to ask her home myself, as a matter of fact.' He sent Dirk a somewhat glowering look, but Dirk didn't appear to notice it.

Meanwhile, it was taken for granted that Matty was to go to Moonak, though she could hardly believe that such an impossibly unacceptable thing had happened. While she ate her steak and let the men talk, she could think of no way of getting out of it. She would have to go to Moonak, that was all.

Half an hour or so later Jerry took his leave.

'I think I'll get back into town and have an early night, now you're fixed up, Matty. I'm not as young as I used to be.' He glanced at Dirk. 'By the way, could I have a word with you about—er—a horse I'm interested in buying?'

'Of course.' Dirk looked surprised, but with a murmured apology he moved off with Jerry. Matty looked after them anxiously. What was Jerry really going to talk to him about? She knew very well he wasn't thinking of buying another horse, so what was he up to?

'Look here, Matty,' Patrick began as the others disappeared. He had opened another can of beer and taken a long drink from it. 'You're going to be my guest at Moonak, not Dirk's. He happened to get in first with the invitation, but that's because he likes to point up the fact that he owns Moonak and I don't. It's his lordly way—and rather hard to take at times. You know what I mean?'

'Yes, I suppose so,' Matty said abstractedly. 'But— would you excuse me a minute, Patrick? I didn't— make arrangements with Jerry about collecting my baggage from the hotel. I must catch him before he goes.'

It was a trumped-up excuse, but Patrick accepted it and she moved off quickly. Though it was dark, she could see Jerry talking earnestly to Dirk not very far from the barbecue and he was so intent on what he was saying that he didn't see her coming. Quite clearly, she heard him saying, 'You can understand why I'd like to see her settled.'

'Don't worry, I'll keep an eye on her,' said Dirk, then he shook Jerry's hand and the two men parted. Matty ran after her uncle who was heading for where his car was parked under the trees.

'Jerry—wait!' she called breathlessly, ignoring Dirk who was going in the other direction. Jerry turned in surprise and stayed where he was. 'I—I just wanted to say I'd have to collect my things from the hotel. But Jerry, what were you saying to Dirk Reasoner about me?'

'Oh, just that you and Patrick seem to hit it off rather well,' he said easily. 'That's true enough, isn't it, Treasure? I could see it the minute I saw the two of you together. That young fellow's nuts about you, Matty ... I told Dirk that I'm not well, as a matter of fact, and that I'm concerned for you, and he's promised to keep an eye on you. I'd like to think there was someone mature and responsible around if anything should happen to me.'

Matty felt a pang of fear. 'I shouldn't leave you, Jerry. I should stay with you—look after you.'

'Now don't fuss, Matty. I won't be going to Ridge Creek on my own. Jim's coming along—he's always done the round with me, and he'll come on to Wanganup too, if I decide to see the whole thing through. That'll depend on what happens at Moonak. To you, I mean,' he said and added with a grin, 'So get cracking, darling, won't you?' They had been walking slowly on and now they had reached his car and he opened the door. 'One other thing I mentioned to Dirk —that your father left you Glenna Downs. It won't hurt for them to know that.'

Matty looked at him speechlessly, but what was the point in reproaches, in protests, now?

'I wanted him to know what sort of background you have,' Jerry explained, excusing himself. 'What's happened isn't your fault, so I don't see why you should suffer for it—any more than I can help. Money doesn't matter to Dirk at any rate.'

'To Dirk?' Matty exclaimed helplessly, but Jerry didn't seem to hear her. She'd thought it was Patrick he was trying to marry her off to, but she didn't know what went on in his mind—any more than he knew what was going on in hers! What a hopeless mess it all was! But her hands were tied. She couldn't upset him by arguing with him, by pulling out.

'Now don't let slip anything that will make a liar

of me, Treasure, will you?' he was saying. He leaned forward and kissed her cheek. 'Dirk'll bring you in to the hotel for your belongings. Have a lovely time, won't you, and see what you can do for yourself. You can give me a full report when you come in for the Ridge Creek races on Wednesday. Right?'

Matty nodded. But as she made her way back to Patrick, she discovered that her faith in her uncle had taken another knock. More and more she realised how little she knew of him as a man. His losing her fortune —if one could call it that—was one thing, but deliberately giving anyone to understand she was still in possession of that fortune—that was something else again. Of course, it would be assumed later that she hadn't known what had happened, and Matty was beginning to wish that she didn't know—that her uncle had kept his secret. She might have felt a lot more confident while she was a guest at Moonak that way.

CHAPTER FIVE

THEY arrived at Moonak homestead in the small hours of Sunday morning. Patrick had had too many beers at the barbecue. He had been half asleep all the way out in the car—a long dark journey through an invisible country, the headlights of the car picking out nothing more than the pale twisted trunks of trees in the scrub.

Patrick went straight to bed. Dirk showed Matty into a bedroom. As at Bunda Bunda, there were twin beds, but here, it looked almost as though she were expected, because there was a posy of red roses in a small vase on the dressing table, and the rose-sprigged cover on one of the beds had been folded away and a corner of the bedclothes turned down. Rose sprigged curtains, the perfume of violets on the bedlinen—Matty looked about her in bewilderment.

'Who—who got the room ready for me?' she asked dazedly.

'My housekeeper, Ruth Clifford.'

'But how did she know I was coming? Or—or are you expecting someone else?'

'Only you,' said Dirk. 'I told her last night you'd be coming.' He was looking at her enigmatically. Her light brown hair was tousled, her eyes were shadowed, and her blue-green dress was crumpled. She should have changed into jeans, but she hadn't wanted to keep Dirk waiting while she collected her luggage from the hotel. She said now, protestingly, 'But you couldn't have told her I'd be coming. You—you didn't know.'

His mouth curved upwards at one corner. 'Are you serious? You really thought I was going to make a couple of passes at you and then forget you?'

'I don't know what you mean—passes. You only——'

'I only kissed you, caressed you? Isn't that enough for a start? Surely you didn't expect me on your little back verandah last night?'

'Of course I didn't,' she said painfully, her face white with fatigue. She turned her back on him and with unsteady fingers opened the two catches on her suitcase, found her pyjamas and toilet things, and laid them carefully on the bed. He was still in the room behind her and she wished he'd go. She was nervous of being alone with him like this, and their conversation seemed somehow dangerous. She had no idea if the housekeeper slept here or in one of the bungalows she'd noticed crouching as though asleep beyond the garden. For all she knew, Patrick was the only other person in this house, and he had immediately disappeared to bed. The house was as quiet as if it were completely empty, Matty could hear nothing but her own breathing, and her senses were stirred by the fresh violet scent of the sheets.

After a moment she turned to see if Dirk had gone, but of course he was still there, leaning against the wall and watching her darkly, through glittering half-closed eyes.

'What—are you looking at?' she challenged.

'At you. A very pretty girl preparing for bed.'

She bit her lip. 'Then I wish you'd stop staring and go away. I'm not—I'm tired. I can't get to bed till you're out of the room.'

'Are you so modest these days?'

'Yes, I am,' she said furiously, though she was beginning to feel more than a little afraid. Would screaming be any use? And was there anything to scream about—yet? She blinked back sudden tears and clenched her fists.

'Am I tormenting you?' Dirk smiled slightly and moved further into the room. 'I suppose I am. But I can't quite make up my mind whether you're too young to be teased, or not young enough.' He paused looking at her seriously, then told her thoughtfully, 'I've never forgotten my first sight of you, Matty, do you know that? It's stayed in my mind like a melody —like a remembered dream. A little vestal virgin, without a stitch on. With nut-brown hair and long graceful legs——' He stopped and her nostrils flared slightly and her breathing quickened. 'I could hardly believe you'd spent the night with my brother ... Anyhow, sit down. You're shaking like a leaf and I suppose you're tired, but I want to talk to you before we part for the night.'

'What about?' Matty sat down helplessly on the side of the bed, reflecting that there seemed no way she could insist on anything—and at least he'd indicated that they'd be—parting for the night.

Dirk sat down too, straddling the narrow chair that stood in front of the dressing table, one of his arms resting along its back. He looked far too big and masculine for the elegant little chair, and Matty tried not to look at him.

'If you're going to tell me what my uncle said to you, I know,' she remarked nervily. 'I—I know he fished for an invitation here for me, and I know he asked you to keep an eye on me, and I know why ... You were right, he's not well.'

He looked at her for a moment, one dark eye half closed. 'Not well is an understatement—I hope you realise that ... And yes, I agreed to keep an eye on you. I'm keeping an eye on myself at this moment too, by the way. If I weren't, I'd have closed the door and would probably be making love to you in your bed right now. At the very least, I'd be kissing the life out of you. But there's something I want to say before we start on anything like that.'

Matty's face crimsoned and then paled. They

weren't going to start on anything like that—not now, not at any time in the future—and she glanced at the half open door as if to check that it was not locked. For an instant she pictured herself fleeing from the room with Dirk in pursuit—instead of Lance Fitzroy. But somehow she didn't think this big, hard, ugly-handsome man would play it the same way as Lance.

'Look, Matty Segal,' said Dirk. 'You've seen this room was made ready for you. You must know I was going to invite you here well before the time Jerry Bridle cast his line——'

'I wouldn't have come,' she interrupted quickly.

'No?' He looked at her consideringly and she straightened nervously from the half reclining position into which she'd somehow slipped. 'I'm pretty sure you would have, and if you're thinking of covering yourself by making out your acquiescence had something to do with Patrick's arrival, you can forget it. You'd have come—if only because you like making trouble for yourself. Don't forget I saw you in action when you were fifteen—*and* that I was there to witness the nasty mess you were all set to create for yourself at the Fitzroys'.'

Matty gasped. What a distortion of the truth!—seeing how he himself had pestered her more than Lance had.

'Apart from getting mixed up with you, I hardly think I was getting into a mess,' she flared.

He smiled slightly. 'You might change your mind if I tell you I didn't go to bed at all that night at Bunda Bunda. I stayed on watch making sure no one came round the verandah to your bed.'

'No one would have come,' she interrupted fiercely. 'You were wasting your time.'

'Someone did come,' he said flatly. 'Lance—once Alice was safely in bed. It was only to be expected. However, he vanished when he encountered me.'

Matty bit her lip. Was it true? Or was he trying to make a hero of himself? Dirk Reasoner to the rescue? The unexpected thought almost made her smile, but not quite; she was too tensed up to be amused at anything. She wondered if he expected her to say thank you, but she wasn't going to.

'You go round with your eyes half closed, Matty,' he resumed. 'I don't know what the hell you see—but I've come to the conclusion it has little to do with reality ... Oh yes, you'd have come to Moonak all right.'

'But I wouldn't,' she persisted, believing it. 'Never! It's the last place I'd have come to.'

He made a dismissive gesture. 'As you like. Though if you really felt that way you wouldn't be here now. Or are you going to tell me it's all because you and Patrick have found each other again, or some such rubbish?'

No, Matty wasn't going to tell him that, because it wouldn't convince him. But neither was she going to tell him the truth—which was that she'd come out of desperation, because of a promise made to her uncle to try to find herself a husband.

However, she didn't have to tell him that. When she said nothing, Dirk got up and crossed the room, closed the door, then came back silently over the soft carpeting to stand looking down at her.

'I know what's going on, Matty,' he said quietly. 'Your uncle told me. Or at least, he told me as much as it suited him to tell me and I can deduce the rest. He told me about his health, and about his concern for you. As for his hope that you and Patrick might team up, I don't know whether he dreamed that one up for himself or whether you put it into his head. But since it just won't work, I don't particularly care.'

'I don't want you to care,' Matty said belligerently. 'If Patrick and I did—fall in love, it wouldn't have anything to do with you.'

'You mean I'm not my brother's keeper?' He moved abruptly and sat down on the bed only inches away from her, half turned towards her. She moved away from him at once, too much aware of his nearness. 'Well, it still won't work. Patrick's in no position to look after you, so you'd better not fall in love with him. He has no prospects at all at the moment. Think of that.'

'But he does have prospects,' she contradicted him. 'He's jackerooing here. Doesn't that mean that in— well, however many years it takes—he can get a job as overseer or—or manager, on another cattle station?'

'Patrick won't finish his training here. I told you he's on trial—and in fact, I don't want him here. He should be using his brain working for his stepfather— that's where his talent lies, with figures. Not here. Loafing round the homestead, cashing in on the privileges of our blood relationship, when he should be riding out with the cattle.'

'What have you got against him?'

'Nothing. But I prefer to face facts. It might be a good thing if you faced a few, too. Doubtless he's told you he and his girl-friend have quarrelled, but I hope the break isn't final. Lyndal's a nice girl. Admittedly you could trap him without very much trouble— you've more than your fair share of sex appeal. But you'd be catching him on the rebound. And don't give me some spiel about how I broke up your burgeoning love affair four years ago. I know damned well you weren't Romeo and Juliet.'

'If—if you feel this way about me,' said Matty, her face pale, 'I can't think why you invited me here. Wouldn't it have been a lot simpler not to?'

'If I hadn't, Patrick would have.' He looked at her darkly, his eyes hard and unreadable. 'Suppose you become engaged to me. Will that achieve your object?'

Matty's eyes widened in disbelief. She didn't think

she could have heard aright. She must be falling asleep—— Yet she knew very well that she wasn't dreaming that dark face that was so close to her own, those eyes that explored hers, the feverish racing of her own pulses.

'You?' She could hardly speak coherently. 'I—I couldn't possibly——'

'You don't like me,' he said, his long mouth curving cynically.

'You know I don't,' she said huskily—though she had long ago become aware that her feelings towards him weren't nearly as simple as that. She disliked Dirk Reasoner—of course she did. She had disliked him—hated him, in fact—for years. Meeting him again couldn't just—wipe out the past and all her feelings, even though she saw him with new eyes. The fact was, she hadn't reached any conclusion as to what she felt about him now, and with every encounter she became more and more confused. 'Anyhow,' she told him, 'there's Rona Fitzroy.'

'Oh, forget Rona Fitzroy,' he said brusquely. 'She's not my fiancée. And you won't dig anyone else out of my recent past either—no estranged wife or discarded mistress or any other encumbrance ... To say you couldn't possibly is absurd, especially if you want to please your uncle. He's worried about you, and I don't wonder, the strife you get yourself into.'

That wasn't what worried Jerry, as Matty knew—it was what he'd done to her future. But she set her teeth and shook her head. 'I couldn't pretend to be engaged to you.'

'We're not talking about pretence,' he said without amusement. 'If you don't feel it's real, I can help you about that with no trouble at all.'

'How?' she asked unwisely.

For perhaps five seconds they stared at each other, then he said, 'Like this,' and reached for her.

Before she even knew what was happening, she was flat on her back on the bed and his body was half covering hers and his mouth was on her lips. Matty was so taken by surprise she didn't even struggle till it was too late to escape from his sheer male strength. His kiss took everything from her, she had no breath left to fight him and was scarcely conscious of what his fingers were doing to the buttons of her dress—until she felt his hand against her bare flesh, felt him unclip the front fastening of her bra——

Oh God, if Jerry knew this sort of thing was to happen to her at Moonak, he'd have a heart attack, she thought, and heard herself utter a little moan. Dirk raised himself slightly, his eyes going to hers to meet them in a long hot exchange. Then gently and deliberately he brushed the palm of his hand across her breasts, and she felt the unaccustomed thrill of desire run through her. She stared back at him as helplessly as though she couldn't move.

'Matilda Segal,' he said, 'will you marry me?'

Matty closed her eyes. Everything had begun to spin and she knew how crazy all this was. She was lying here, her clothes in a mess, her body partly uncovered, letting him touch her, letting him—yes, letting him do as he liked with her, unresistingly. The wonder was that he wasn't doing more, and with that thought came the realisation that she wasn't safe yet. She struggled to sit up and to pull the edges of her dress together, to re-fasten the buttons. To her relief Dirk didn't stop her, though he didn't help her either, and he looked slightly amused.

'You see,' he said then, his dark eyes enigmatic, 'wouldn't it be just as easy to say yes to me as it would be to Patrick?'

'You don't mean it,' she wanted to say. 'You're not really asking me to marry you. It's all just so that I'll leave your brother alone.' But she didn't say it, and only realised when he handed her a large unfolded white handkerchief that she was crying.

'Mop up your tears,' he said. 'It's all over now.'

What was all over? The joke? She pressed the handkerchief quickly to her eyes and told him, 'If this is supposed to be a—a joke, I'm not amused.'

'It's not a joke, so you don't need to be amused. You needn't be too frightened either. I'm not going to make love to you, much as I'd like to. You can answer the question I just asked you tomorrow. Think it over before you go to sleep—try to see the sense in it. Think how pleased your uncle will be, how much more pleased than if it were Patrick, and I had to warn him that Patrick can offer you nothing.'

Matty felt too choked to make any sort of an answer. One part of her wanted to tell him he'd have to half kill her before she'd marry him, but some other crazy side of her nature wanted to say yes—and she couldn't think why, except—except that Jerry *would* be pleased. That was an undisputable fact.

When he left her a minute later with a murmured remark about sleeping well, she got up from the bed and staggered to the mirror to reassure herself that she was still Matty Segal, and she was still intact. What had Jerry said? That no one would have much trouble falling in love with her. But Dirk Reasoner hadn't done that. He was simply—protecting his brother and, presumably, Patrick's girl-friend too. Matty pressed a hand to her cheek. She didn't want to marry anyone, she told herself. Oh yes, she'd made up her mind she'd get engaged—to *someone*—to make Jerry happy, though actually she supposed she hadn't really believed it would happen.

And now she had a proposal of marriage—from the most unlikely person in the world. Dirk Reasoner.

Think it over.

She stared at her reflection—the pale face, the

golden freckles across her nose, her mouth—soft, vulnerable, slightly swollen from the pressure of a man's lips. She looked at her disordered hair and then down at the front opening of her dress, the buttons she had fumbled with done up wrongly. Automatically she undid them and the dress fell open to reveal her bare bosom. He had—touched her again, looked at her nakedness. He was the only man who had ever come so close to her. Matty could almost hear her own heartbeats as she turned away from the mirror and began to undress.

She couldn't possibly tell Dirk Reasoner that she'd marry him. It was—it was ludicrous. It was not even to be considered. So why was she considering it? Think how pleased your uncle will be, he'd said. And of course Jerry would be delighted. But all the same——

By morning, she'd decided she'd do it. Not marry him, of course—just get engaged. It was the right thing, at least as far as Jerry was concerned. She was sure of it. He'd—he'd forgive himself his transgressions because everything was going to be all right for Matty after all. He'd be able to die happy. It was a sombre thought.

Late though she'd been to bed, Dirk woke her early, calling through the door to ask her if she'd like to go out riding with him. Patrick was still in bed. 'Too much beer last night,' Dirk said, and added offhandedly, 'Drowning his sorrows.'

This morning he treated Matty impersonally when she came out to the kitchen where he was making toast on the electric toaster. It was Sunday, and she gathered that the housekeeper had at least the morning off. No one would ever guess, Matty thought, what had happened in her room in the small hours of the morning, to see them together now, though every time her eyes met his she felt a shiver go through her.

'You do ride, don't you?' he asked her as she sat

down at the table and poured herself a cup of coffee, leaving the toast-making to him. The homestead, she had discovered, was comfortable and unpretentious— and big. Not as big as the Fitzroys' place, probably, and certainly not as showy, but then Dirk had no wife to take a pride in it. The kitchen and bathrooms were up to date, and though there was no air-conditioning, there were fans in the ceilings of most of the rooms, and from the verandah she had glimpsed the glittering water of a swimming pool, behind a group of palms.

'Yes, I ride,' she told him in answer to his question. She was sure he must have wakened her early so that they could be alone and that he probably had the same purpose in mind when he asked her to go out riding with him. He'd want to know what she'd decided about marrying him, of course. He wasn't the sort of man who'd let it hang fire—he'd push her till she answered him. Well, she'd made up her mind and she'd have to get it over. The thing was, she couldn't very well tell him she intended their engagement to be only a temporary measure, or that she had no intention of marrying him. But surely he wouldn't seduce her— surely he wasn't as uncivilised, as unprincipled, as that. She glanced across the table at his dark face and unreadable eyes, and admitted to herself that he very easily could be.

'I want to have a look at some fencing that's in progress,' he told her later as they left the house together. 'I don't usually work on Sundays, but during race week most of the men are in town, so I like to check up.'

'Why don't you—rouse the jackeroo, then?' Matty asked a little facetiously. 'Doesn't he like riding too, anyhow?'

Dirk shrugged. 'I wouldn't say it was Patrick's favourite pastime. And since he hasn't bothered to get up off his backside yet, he can stay in bed.'

Matty said no more. It was plainer than ever to her that he didn't want Patrick to have anything to do with Moonak.

It was exhilarating riding out over the vast paddocks of long grasses and scattered scrub. Matty hadn't been on horseback since she was twelve, and now she revelled in it all—in the feel of the horse beneath her, in the air, already growing hot, that lifted her hair back from her forehead, in the sights and sounds of a countryside that was very different from the Darling Downs. Soon they were riding by a river that held water, unlike many of the rivers of the west, and was fringed with melaleucas and acacias and gum trees. High in the branches, noisy galahs clowned about as if they had the world to themselves, their breasts flashing rose pink, their wings silver-grey. The pale beautiful stretches of straw-coloured grasses were broken by dark clumps of trees, and on the horizon were long red mesas, their edges blotted by the shimmering amethyst of a growing heat haze.

The fencing work that was in progress had been abandoned during race week, and Matty saw the gleaming silver of new wire making a three-strand fence—to hold the cattle in special paddocks when the stock muster began, Dirk said.

'Some of Moonak's ten thousand square kilometres are practically inaccessible except on horseback. I use a helicopter to hunt the cattle out of the wild country on to the flats, where my stockmen can take over. My overseer looks after the southern end of the run—it borders almost on the edge of the Great Sandy Desert, did you know that?'

Matty didn't, and she was fascinated, and when Dirk rode ahead of her she watched him thoughtfully —and presently caught herself out wondering what it would be like to be married to him. Somehow it wasn't such a daunting prospect as she looked at his broad muscular back, the gleaming darkness of his thick hair, the superb way he sat his horse. But when he was looking at her—that was different. She remembered then the muscular strength it was impossible to struggle against, the bruising pressure of his lips on hers. How many women had he made love to? Patrick had said he brought girls to his flat in Perth. Did he still do that? Would he still do it if he were married —to her? But it would never come to that. An engagement could easily be broken, she assured herself. If only Jerry hadn't messed around with her money—if only he weren't so ill—she wouldn't be in this predicament. She wouldn't feel forced to do something that was so utterly distasteful to her. As it was, she couldn't turn her back, refuse to take this opportunity to relieve his mind.

Worrying a little, she waited in the shade while Dirk dismounted and went to inspect a windmill, a tank, a trough where cattle were drinking.

'Water's all-important in this country,' he remarked when he came back. 'Cattle drink at least forty litres of water a day each, so it's got to be there.'

As they rode back to the homestead, he slowed his horse to keep pace with hers so that he could talk to her. He hadn't mentioned his proposal so far, but now he was sure to, and she felt herself wavering. 'You've got to say yes,' she told herself. 'Think of Jerry.'

'You ride well,' he said. 'Where—and when—did you learn?'

'When I was a child. I—my father ran cattle on the Darling Downs.'

'Ah yes, Jerry Bridle told me something about that. On Glenna Downs, wasn't it? And your father left the property to you.'

'No, he—he left it to my mother,' she said nervously. 'I was only twelve when he died, and we came over to

Perth. We didn't have any relatives in Queensland after Jerry left there and came to the West. He was my mother's only brother. She—died—quite suddenly. We'd only been in Perth about a month.'

Dirk listened thoughtfully but he didn't offer her any sympathy, and after a moment asked, 'Who's running the property for you, Matty?'

She looked at him quickly. 'Oh, my mother sold out and—er—invested the money. I told you it wasn't left to me. You must have been mistaken if you got the idea it was.'

'All right, then let's not make a song and dance about it ... Your uncle looked after the investments for you, did he? I recall you saying the other day he looked after your affairs.'

Uncomfortably, Matty glanced away at the tangle of purple shadows that made weird patterns among the mulgas through which they were riding. Why did he have to ask all these embarrassing questions? She didn't see he had any right. It wasn't as if she were his fiancée yet, and for all he knew, she might have decided to turn him down. Though somewhere in her heart she knew with a kind of excitement that was half dread that he wasn't in any doubt as to what her answer would be—that if she didn't give in and say yes right away, then he'd soon work her round to saying it. And the methods he'd use were those he'd tried last night, to show her there'd be no pretence. 'Why me?' she wondered. *Was* it so she'd leave Patrick alone —or so Patrick would have to leave *her* alone, more correctly. Though of course Dirk knew she was supposed to be looking for someone to take care of her when her uncle was gone. One thing only was as clear as daylight, and that was that he didn't—couldn't— love her.

'Well?' he was saying insistently, and she told him

reluctantly, 'Yes. My mother asked Jerry to be my guardian before she died.'

'I see. Then I hope he didn't put your money into racehorses. I have an idea he made a few very ill-fated investments in that field on his own behalf not many years ago. Isn't that so?'

'I wouldn't have a clue,' Matty said stiffly. 'He never discussed his business with me—I was only a school-girl.'

'Did your mother know he was a gambler?' he asked unexpectedly, and she flushed.

'He wasn't. He—he gave it up, before he married. So don't—don't try to tell me anything against my uncle.'

'I'm not doing that. I was merely referring to something I believe to be a fact. I take it you're perfectly satisfied with the way he runs your affairs, then.'

'Of course I am,' said Matty. It would have been perfectly true such a short time ago, now it was a lie, but there was no way she could avoid telling an un-truth. 'I've always had everything I wanted,' she hur-ried on. 'I—I did go to the same school as Rona Fitz-roy, you know.'

His mouth twisted in a wry smile. 'You don't have to press the point. Patrick told me that years ago— I'm not questioning your truthfulness.'

'And I'd have had a trip to Europe this year if my aunt hadn't died,' Matty added, anxious to convince him of her trust in Jerry.

'Oh yes,' he said thoughtfully. 'I see now why you were so sure your uncle wouldn't have had to sell Waltzing Matilda to finance that. Your own money would have paid for it.'

'Yes ... Do you want to ask me any more questions?' she demanded, her cheeks flushed.

'Only one,' he said. 'Are you going to marry me?'

Oh God! It was crazy, but hearing him say it again sent a shock through her heart. This was the moment when she was supposed to say yes, and it wasn't easy. 'Jerry will be so pleased,' she reminded herself desperately. 'It can be a long engagement—we don't need to set a date for the wedding.' Surely it was quite safe to say yes.

They had both reined in in the shade of the mulgas, and she looked at Dirk covertly and knew that it wasn't quite safe. How could she stop him making love to her? She hadn't been able to do a thing last night. But—but once it was all signed and sealed, so to speak, couldn't she explain that she wanted to be with Jerry—stay in Ridge Creek after the Wednesday race meeting? If there really was no spare room at the hotel, there surely must be somewhere else she could stay—anywhere, so long as she didn't have to come back to Moonak.

'Why the reluctance?' he asked when two or three minutes had gone by and she had said nothing. 'You want someone to look after you, don't you? And I'm sure Jerry Bridle will have no objections when you tell him it's me you're planning to marry, and not Patrick. You could search longer and fare a lot worse, you know. Or are you disappointed Moonak's not as impressive as the Fitzroys' homestead? It can be redecorated—to your own personal taste——'

'I—I don't care about redecorating. And if you'd stop getting at me'—she paused and drew a deep breath—'I was going to say yes.' It was out—she'd actually said it, and she looked at him through her lashes to see his reaction. He was studying her, his expression quizzical.

'Are you sure?'

Matty nodded. Oh yes, she was sure it was the only thing to do. She was also sure she was a fool, she thought suddenly, for her heart had begun to beat madly and she had the sudden crazy desire to have him take her in his arms and kiss her and——

'You don't think you're asking for trouble?'

Of course she was! If ever a girl was asking for trouble it was Matty Segal. But she wasn't going to marry him—she wasn't as mad as that. Yet even so at this moment she was dimly aware that she was heading for bigger trouble than she'd ever been in during the whole of her life.

She gave her mare a smart tap in the rump and galloped off through the scrub, leaving Dirk to follow her.

CHAPTER SIX

THEY arrived back at the homestead in the midday heat to be greeted on the verandah by a resentful Patrick, wanting to know where they'd been and why Matty had gone without him.

Dirk cut in to tell him with brutal bluntness, 'You'd better forget any ideas you may have had of using Matty as a poultice for your broken heart, Patrick. She's just agreed to marry me.' He sent Matty a dark look as he spoke, a look that made her pulses jump and her heart race. He didn't touch her, but that single glance did more to her senses than the pressure of his fingers on her wrist or shoulder would have done.

Patrick was staring incredulously from one to the other of them.

'What *is* this?' he demanded. 'You've just got to be joking! Matty's *my* guest, Dirk, even if you handed out the invitation. Come on, now, you're having me on——'

'We're not having you on, and I'm not joking. Nor was there ever any question of Matty's being your guest.'

'Oh, so it's a case of the old bull having first pick of the cows, is it?' Patrick said aggressively.

Matty stood there feeling—oh, she didn't know how she felt. As if she'd stepped into some play that just didn't make sense and had no logic in it. She couldn't blame Patrick for not believing she and Dirk were engaged. Absolutely nothing had been said to prepare him for it, and even she was having difficulty in believing it was true. Once again she had a sense of confusion and bewilderment. What had she done? She clenched her fists and repeated to herself words that were becoming a rote: *Jerry will be pleased.* But that didn't any longer make it seem either right or real.

Dirk was saying, 'You can keep that kind of remark to yourself, Patrick. It's not only crass and immature, it's also asking for a punch up the nose.'

'Oh, please!' Matty interjected. Then discovering to her dismay that she was about to burst into tears, she turned away and hurried inside. Nobody came after her, and she closed the door of her bedroom with a bang. But instead of flinging herself face down on the bed and crying into her pillow—which she felt very much like doing—she wiped her eyes angrily and began rather vigorously to make her bed, which she hadn't had time to do earlier in the morning.

Now she *was* in a mess—one of those messes Dirk had claimed she had such a propensity for getting into. She really was, this time, oh heavens! she had to get through two more whole days after this one before she could disappear to Ridge Creek.

At last, having straightened the bedspread, she moved to the mirror and stared at her reflection with bewildered eyes. She couldn't just disappear from Moonak and she knew it. Jerry was hardly likely to believe in her engagement that way, was he? She began to feel oddly frightened. What was the matter with her? What *did* she want? She didn't know—or if she knew, then she wasn't ready to face it.

She sat down on the little slender chair where Dirk had sat last night and pulled her boots off. She found her sandals, but instead of putting them on, she decided to take a shower. By the time she'd done that and got into a fresh cool dress, she might be feeling better. And those two she had left on the verandah might have quietened down. She couldn't really see that Patrick had any right to be unpleasant about

what had happened. After all, he might have turned
up here with his girl-friend and not cared a fig
whether she got engaged to his brother or to the—the
King of the Barbaroos!

Matty sighed and gave up.

A long shower helped, and so did washing her hair
and getting into a cotton knit dress with a motif of
pale water-green rushes printed on a neutral background. Aware that she must face the situation—and
the men—some time, she made her way slowly along
the hall. Where were they now? She heard voices from
the dining room, the clink of glasses, Patrick's voice.

'How could I know you had that sort of thing in
mind? When did you meet her? A week ago——'

Oh dear, they were still talking about her. Matty
almost went back to her room, but she wanted to hear
what they said, so she stayed where she was and listened.

'I met her four years ago,' said Dirk. 'That gave me
a head start.'

'Oh no, not on me!' There was something unpleasant in the way Patrick said that, and Matty bit her lip.
She knew what he was insinuating, and it wasn't fair—
it really wasn't.

'Quit big-noting yourself,' Dirk said dryly. 'You were
hardly a Don Juan at seventeen. Besides, you'd emptied
my whisky bottle, and I know damned well you were
too drunk to make love to anyone but a practised
whore. You didn't take that girl's virginity. Be adult
about it—forget her, make it up with Lyndal——'

'Lyndal's pushing the same barrow you are—nagging
at me to go into the family firm. I'm not going to be
part of a twosome where the woman wears the pants.'

'Okay, then find yourself another girl. But if I catch
you trying anything on with Matty I'll——'

Matty didn't listen any more. Silently she fled to her

bedroom and didn't reappear until Dirk called out that lunch was ready.

It appeared that Ruth Clifford had been busy in the kitchen while she and Dirk were out riding, because a salad and cold meats were on the table which was laid for three. It was a strained meal, with conversation at a minimum, and when Patrick asked her before they left the table if she'd like a swim in the pool later on, she said politely, 'No, thank you—I think I'd rather have a rest.'

In actual fact, she slept most of the afternoon, and woke a little before five feeling hot and sticky. She got off the bed and went to the window to look out at a world that was somnolent with heat. The bright clarity of the sun had gone, and the garden had a dull coppery sheen over it. It looked sizzling. There must be dust in the air, she thought. The temptation to cool off in the tiled pool among its green palms was too much to resist. She'd heard Dirk's half threat to Patrick, and she didn't want to make trouble, but to go and swim now of her own choice was hardly putting him in the wrong.

She got out of the slip that was all she'd worn while she rested and put on her swimsuit. It was a pale jade green, soft and light with no stiff bra cups. She didn't bother with a towel, but put on sandals and her sunglasses and started off across the garden. She'd gone only a few yards when she encountered Dirk, whose eyes skimmed over her as his brows came down frowningly.

'Go and get a shirt on,' he told her. 'We're going out in the jeep.'

'What?' Matty exclaimed. 'But I—I want a swim. I was going out to the pool.'

'You'll have your swim,' he said, 'but not in the pool. So do as I tell you.'

'But what if I don't want to go out in the jeep?' she protested, resenting his domineering attitude.

His eyes narrowed. 'Are you implying you'd sooner spend the next couple of hours with Patrick?'

'Patrick doesn't come into it.'

'Oh yes, he does. He's out there on one of the loungers. And if you want to know why we don't go and join him, it's for two reasons. One, I want you to myself, and two, I'd like you to know a little more about Moonak. The more primitive aspects, not the civilised touches.'

Matty said no more. Wordlessly she turned and went back to her room. What did the primitive aspects of Moonak have to do with her? She'd never be living here. All the same, she did as he told her and slipped into a checked, button-fronted shirt.

'There are towels in the jeep,' Dirk told her when she rejoined him. The jeep was already on the drive, and Matty wondered if Dirk had been waiting for some time before she woke for her to emerge from her room.

It was a rough ride out to the river in the jeep, and, beyond asking if she felt better after her rest, Dirk hadn't much to say. He took her to a place where there was a deep pool shaded by willows and melaleucas, though even there the insistent heat of the sun penetrated, coming down from a hot sky that seemed gauzed with copper. Matty still simmered with resentment, and instead of stripping off her shirt, she got out of the jeep and stood under the trees looking down at the water, brushing away an occasional fly, and absentmindedly pulling pieces of soft papery bark from the tree trunk.

'What's the matter? Are you thinking how much nicer it would have been at the homestead?' Dirk spoke from a few feet away. He had discarded shirt and pants and was wearing black trunks. It was the first time she'd seen him stripped down like this and despite herself her eyes were drawn to his broad shoulders, his narrow hips and muscular thighs. Her eyes followed unwillingly yet as if compelled the dark hair that made a triangle on his tanned chest, then thinned to a line that went down to his navel and continued across his flat, hard-looking belly. Colour suffused her cheeks when she found him watching her, his mouth quirking in amusement.

'Well?' he said enigmatically, and her colour deepened.

'Well—what?' she said huskily, and almost expected him to ask what she thought of him after that detailed appraisal of his very masculine body.

He raised his eyebrows. 'Are you thinking of the attractions of the homestead pool?'

Of course she wasn't thinking of that, and she was sure he knew it. Disconcerted, she unbuttoned her shirt, took it off and tossed it on the ground, then without a word ran down the hot purplish gravel and plunged into the water. It was cooler than she had expected, and she submerged several times, then pushed back her hair and began to swim, ignoring Dirk who had joined her in the water and was swimming with powerful strokes to the other side of the pool.

After perhaps fifteen minutes Matty left the water, and with her back turned to it, she rubbed her hair dry on one of the towels Dirk had brought from the jeep. She watched a stream of birds flowing across the sky that was now flushing to a hot burnt orange—a sky such as she had never seen before, its colours sending a glow up from the earth so that she felt she was standing on heated copper. She remembered what Dirk had said about the Great Sandy Desert fringing on Moonak's southern boundary, and she felt a stirring of restlessness, of nostalgia—as if there was something here that belonged to her.

When Dirk left the water a few minutes later he didn't bother with a towel, but having pressed some of the water from his thick dark hair, came to stand near Matty and leave it to the air to dry his body.

'I hope you took no notice of Patrick's attitude,' he remarked, as if continuing a conversation. 'I assure you you've done no damage to his heart. It's just that he likes to have his own way. My mother—his mother—has been too lenient with him. She has something of a guilt complex where he's concerned, and he's inclined to play on it.'

'A guilt complex? Why should she have that?' Matty wanted to know. She hadn't expected him to talk about Patrick, and she reflected wryly that his assurances were not exactly flattering—and doubtless were not meant to be! She picked up her shirt and put it on self-consciously. Even though her swimsuit covered her decently, it showed too much of the shape of her body, and she was aware that Dirk's eyes, dark in their setting of black, water-sharpened lashes, were on her while he was talking of other things. They were very sexy eyes, she thought suddenly, and she wondered how many girls he had watched dressing—or undressing. In that flat in Perth. Or even here—in this secluded place on the river ...

'Patrick hasn't told you about his mother?' he was asking, and she shook her head. 'Well, I'll tell you, because you seem to have the mistaken idea I'm keeping him from his rightful inheritance. The plain fact is, my father sent my mother away to Perth five or six months before Patrick was born. Their marriage had been virtually over for some time, but all the same he made her a generous allowance and saw that she was well looked after during her pregnancy and later on. The divorce went through, and he supported her and Patrick fully right up to the time the kid was five years old and she married Bob Dean, who adopted him legally.'

Matty didn't fully understand. 'But—Patrick was—was his son——'

'My father's? Or do you mean Bob Dean's? No. Patrick's father was a geologist who stayed at the homestead for about two weeks and then went merrily on his way. My mother, in other words, cuckolded my father. Or would you prefer me to put it more romantically and say she had a brief encounter? In either case, the end result was the same. And I have the greatest sympathy with any man who prefers not to accept responsibility for a child in such circumstances. If you like dabbling your toes in psychopathology, Matty—and if you've wondered about my bachelor state—you might make a few deductions from what I've told you. I don't indulge in mental dissection myself, I'd rather use common sense. But I do know that at thirteen I didn't want my mother to go out of my life, and I guess I thought she might be allowed to stay around for my sake. None the less, I learned then that you can't trust women—the pretty ones probably least of all.'

A little troubled, Matty raised clear eyes to his. 'I think you're carrying it too far. Oh, I suppose as a child you must have been hurt and disillusioned. But you can't judge all women by one. You—you've been around, after all, haven't you?'

'Sure I have,' he agreed sardonically. 'And my eyes are very wide open. But are you by any chance suggesting that you're dependable—trustworthy? In your relationships with men, I mean. To be specific—with me.' He moved a few steps nearer as he spoke and her eyes fell before the look in his and became rivetted on his diaphragm, where drops of water still glistened. She felt herself flush slowly, guiltily, because she knew

she wasn't trustworthy. She'd said she'd marry him—
but she had no intention of doing so.

'What would be your reaction,' he asked, 'if I spread
out that beach towel that's lying at your feet, and
pulled you down on the ground and made love to you?
Now.'

Matty licked lips that were suddenly dry, and shivered slightly despite the heat. 'You—you wouldn't,' she
faltered. 'You have no right——'

'No right? Isn't that an odd attitude to take when
you told me only this morning that you'd marry me?
If you really meant it, you'd want my arms around
you—you'd want me to teach you more of the pleasures
of lovemaking than that little bit of loveplay I
taught you last night.'

Last night—only last night! Matty's mind darted
back quickly, then recoiled in fright at what it encountered—the memory of his body over hers, his
hand on her naked breast, her awareness of his stirring
passion and of her own. And now he was standing too
close to her and the thought of being clasped to his
almost naked body did strange things to her. Her chest
felt strangely constricted, and she was scarcely able to
breathe.

'Oh no, darling,' he said cynically into the little
silence that had fallen between them. 'I don't trust
you. I know damn well you have no intention of
marrying me—that your one and only idea is to make
your uncle happy. By fooling him,' he finished significantly.

'Then—then why did you ask me?' she stammered,
as if to point out that hers was not the only blame.

'To help you out,' he said—and added, 'Among
other things ... But don't imagine I'm prepared to
make a pact with you. I'm not. You've agreed to marry
me, and as far as I'm concerned that's it.' He was looking at her hard, his dark eyes glittering through the

black lashes, and she felt herself shiver inwardly. There was something—uncivilised about his regard, and the mad thought came into her mind that he was showing her the primitive side of himself, as well as that of his cattle run.

'But take comfort from this,' he resumed, his gaze settling on her mouth, 'I've never yet made love to a woman who didn't want it.'

'Well, I—*I* don't want it,' Matty got out unsteadily.

She heard his brief laugh as he suddenly seized her wrist and with a swift movement hauled her to him, bringing the softness of her body into such violent contact with his own muscled hardness that she was almost winded. Her instinct was to fight, but his hands held her prisoner, and her feeble struggles got her nowhere. He bent his head and kissed her mouth, urging her lips apart, and in seconds she had ceased to resist. Her lips parted, the protest in her mind vanished, and the sensations of her body took over completely. Her fingers sought the roughness of his chest and she was excruciatingly aware that one of his hands had slipped down to low on her spine so he could hold her even closer against him. She felt a sweet sickness invade her, and she knew that if he were to draw her down on the ground with him now, she wouldn't resist. She wanted him—just as much as he seemed to want her.

He slid his other hand inside her unbuttoned shirt and over the silky smoothness of her almost dry swimsuit, till it came to rest caressingly against the palpitating curve of her breast.

'You want me to be your lover, don't you?' he said huskily against her still parted lips.

She couldn't answer. Her body was alive with desire, and she struggled with herself for sanity. To be carried away like this—without the least effort on his part—it was—humiliating, and yet she knew that if he wanted to go on, she would give way. She was achingly consci-

ous of her sexual hunger and of his, and even now she
wanted his mouth back on hers, his lips exciting her.
But he was more in command of his reactions than she
was of hers, and instead of pressing her for an answer,
instead of kissing her again—instead of following the
way passion was leading them, he released her slightly,
withdrawing his hips from hers, but still holding her
steady. She lowered her head till her brow lay against
his bare skin and forced herself to draw a long slow
breath, to exhale, to breathe in again. She knew she
should be thankful he hadn't forced her on, and as she
gained more control over herself she felt deeply
ashamed that she had betrayed such weakness.

Presently she stepped away from him, stooped for
the towel she had dropped, and without speaking made
her way back to the jeep. Her steps were unsteady and
her body was still tormented. What trap had she
allowed herself to be caught in? And how on earth
could she ever hope to escape from it unscathed? And
did she—did she want to? a flash of painful honesty
made her ask herself.

It was minutes before he joined her in the jeep, and
then, instead of saying mockingly, as she half expected
him to, 'So you don't want me to make love to you?'
he merely asked, 'Are you all right, Matty?'

She nodded, the sudden sting of tears in her eyes,
but she couldn't look at him. And despite her mortifi-
cation, as he turned the jeep and they began the
bumpy ride back to the homestead, she was disturbingly
aware of him and of the excitement his mere nearness
stirred in her. She'd thought she'd want to run away
from him—to hide—to be alone, but she didn't. *Here*
was where she wanted to be—next to this unpredict-
able domineering male, waiting with thumping heart
for what he'd do—or say—next. It was as though he'd
added something to her life that had been missing before, and that now she couldn't do without.

Added what? she asked herself somberly, and risked a glance at him through her lashes—then caught her breath. That hard dark face, that hint of ugliness that added a spice to his good looks. Because, heaven help her, he *was* good-looking, and she was amazed she hadn't realised it before. It was incredible that until a few short days ago her experience of him had been limited to one brief—but searing—encounter. Since then she'd agreed to marry him, without the least intention of doing so. And now it seemed he was fully aware of her duplicity and was prepared to trample her wants into the dust and have his own way. Why, she didn't know. But she was beginning to wonder fearfully if she'd have to go ahead and marry him. At the rate she was going, she reflected wryly, she probably would. So was it the mere excitement of sex she was no longer prepared to live without? That was hardly a good foundation for marriage. Sex—not love. And no matter what Jerry had said about love, Matty was convinced there was something special—something spontaneous and beautiful and spiritual—in the love between a man and a woman. If it really was love.

She certainly didn't love Dirk Reasoner, and she glanced at him uneasily as they reached the homestead.

'What's been keeping you so deep in thought?' he asked casually, and she felt a curious stab at her heart as he looked into her eyes.

'Nothing,' she said inadequately.

'Nothing? I rather thought you might have found food for contemplation in one or two things that happened this afternoon.'

'Such as?' Matty asked, as the jeep came to a standstill and she clambered out.

'Such as that our engagement isn't going to be the thing of pretence that you imagined. And that you don't dislike me as much as you make out.'

'But I do dislike you,' she said, her colour high.

'Only you have—brute strength on your side, don't you?'

He narrowed his dark eyes. 'Would you like me better without it?' he asked ironically.

Matty turned away in confusion ...

Dirk and Patrick went out in the jeep next morning and Matty was left to put in the day as best she could. They didn't leave until after she'd breakfasted, and from the shade of the verandah she watched them drive off—two very masculine men going off into a man's world. She simply hadn't been asked along. How, she wondered, after the—passion of the day before, could Dirk simply walk out on her? It was incomprehensible and definitely unflattering. She was apparently expected to content herself with the company of the housekeeper, Ruth Clifford, a handsome, rather hearty countrywoman with broad hips and a cheerful disposition, whom she had at last met over breakfast. 'My fiancée,' Dirk had said casually as he introduced them, and though a spark of surprise showed in the housekeeper's eyes, she didn't ask any questions.

Coming into the house after the jeep had disappeared, Matty glanced at her watch. A whole empty day lay ahead of her, and though she tried to tell herself she was thankful, she knew she wasn't. It was as though she needed the irritant of Dirk's presence. She wanted a continuation of what had been happening yesterday—a continuation of the struggle between them. His telling her so coolly that he wasn't prepared to make a pact with her had her on edge. Did he really think he could compel her to marry him, regardless of her feelings? Well, he was in for a shock, because she wasn't coming back to Moonak after the races on Wednesday. Being engaged didn't mean she had to stay here. She'd insist that Jerry needed her with him. Dirk knew Jerry was ill—he couldn't deny him her company. She certainly wasn't going to stay here and have Dirk compromise her, force her into a submission she didn't really want. No way could she see herself as Dirk Reasoner's wife. No way? a treacherous voice inside her whispered.

She had reached her room and obeying some subconscious impulse she took from her suitcase the two dresses that Rona had ripped. Now as she examined them, one part of her mind was telling her it would be hopeless to try to repair the damage, and another part was still preoccupied with Dirk Reasoner—with the impossible notion of Matilda Segal becoming Matilda Reasoner.

With his body he would love her.

Matty bit her lip and shook her head as if to clear it. You don't marry a man just because he has the ability to stir you up sexually—*or* because he says so. Somehow she'd persuade him to see things her way, out of consideration for a sick man.

She tidied her room, then borrowed a sewing kit from Ruth Clifford and taking her black and tan silk dress on to the verandah, began mending it. The necessity to concentrate and to make tiny stitches absorbed her mind, and she began to feel quite a sense of achievement in her careful work. After all, Matty Segal as from now had to learn to be thrifty. She couldn't, as she once would have done, simply discard her dress and whizz off to town and buy a new one.

During the morning a pretty aboriginal girl—there appeared to be two or three of them helping in the house—brought her a small jug of ice-cold lemon squash and some home-made biscuits, and by the time she'd finished mending her dress it was lunchtime. It was certainly nice to be waited on, to have a tempting meal served to her at a small table on a shady part of the verandah, because the day was so hot she was totally devoid of energy. She ate with enjoyment, and drank two cups of weak tea with lemon, and after that was content to stagger to her room where she took off most of her clothes, collapsed on the bed, and slept for two hours.

She had been swimming, but was sprawled out by the pool when the two men came home. Patrick apparently went straight inside, but Dirk came to find Matty, and her heartbeat accelerated as she watched him striding through the palms towards her. He looked tough and hard in black pants, a red and black checked shirt, and a black neckerchief. His face, his boots, his clothes were filmed with reddish dust, and he looked like a stockman. Matty had never seen this aspect of him. She'd always known he was hard, but this way he looked infinitely more so. The kind of man you couldn't win against, who'd ruthlessly take what he wanted——

As she lay on the lounger in the shade of the palms, she felt his eyes moving over her exploringly and she longed to reach down for her towel and cover herself. He'd be mockingly amused if she did that, of course —he'd seen every part of her naked body four years ago, her swimsuit didn't hide anything he didn't know about. Her thoughts were disturbing her, and she asked him jerkily, 'What have you been doing today?'

'Various things. Looking for an open gate and finding a break in the paddock fence. Hunting out stock that were where they shouldn't have been. Mending the fence.' He spoke prosaically, and sat down in one of the fibreglass chairs that stood on the grass, sending her a dark-eyed half smile that sent shivers up and down her spine.

'*You* mended the fence?' she said idiotically. 'I'd have thought you employed someone to do such things.'

'Would you?' His eyebrows rose lazily. 'Well, so I do, but it's race week, remember. And in any case I'm more interested in keeping everything on my property in good order than in playing the big boss. I was born the son of a cattleman, but I wasn't brought up either idle or ignorant. I learned station management—animal husbandry, book-keeping—the lot, anyhow, and I learned it in a practical way. I also served an apprenticeship in well sinking, and in putting up windmills, and doing fencing. Are you surprised? Did you think my life was one long holiday, that I spend my time going to house parties and proposing marriage to attractive young women?'

Matty flushed. 'If you really want to know, I haven't thought about you at all,' she said with a total disregard for the truth.

He gave her a crooked smile. 'That's a lie,' he said flatly. 'I'll bet you've spent half today thinking about me.'

'Well, I didn't,' said Matty, flushing. 'You may have come into my head once or twice, like a—like a mosquito or something, but I was busy.'

'Doing what?' He seemed amused rather than annoyed, and she was positive he was unconvinced.

'Swimming—mending my dress——'

'The one that was damaged at Bunda Bunda? Well, it's nice to know you have a few useful skills too. Most girls as fortunate as you are would have tossed it out —given it to the mission girls. Used it as an excuse to buy something new next trip down to Perth.'

'I didn't bring all that many dresses with me,' Matty shrugged. 'And I don't know exactly when Jerry and I shall be going back to Perth.'

'I imagine your uncle will be going fairly soon, from what he told me. Once he's satisfied your future is more or less assured he won't waste his time or his strength attending any more race meetings,' Dirk said positively. 'I gather he wants to get his affairs into order ... But you won't be going with him, Matty, you'll be staying here with me. I'll take you down to Perth a little later when we've settled our wedding date. Would you like to be married in Perth?' he finished deliberately.

Matty, who had been looking at the blue-green waters of the pool, turned her head sharply and met his eyes. He referred to their wedding as if there were no argument about it, and yet he knew perfectly well she didn't want to marry him. She said tautly, 'I think we'd better call our engagement off. Nobody knows about it except Patrick. And I don't—I don't want to marry you.'

He gave her a long straight look, then drawled, 'You'll have time to change you mind about that, darling. Because I'm definitely not allowing you to back out. Just think how *you'd* feel if some attractive male was going to marry you and then told you to forget about it, it was all off. That, with the male and female roles reversed, is what you're trying to do to me, and I don't take kindly to it. On Wednesday I intend to let everyone know of our engagement. You can mopoke all you like, you're going to stick to your agreement.'

'Oh!' Matty slid her feet to the grass and stood up. 'You—you're impossible! You know my uncle's sick—that he's worried about me. You—you know why I said I'd marry you.'

'I'm afraid you're a bit too late with your honesty. If you merely wanted my connivance in tricking your uncle you should have told me much much sooner. At all events, I'm not convinced by your protests. Do you want to know why?'

'No, thank you,' said Matty, and snatched up her towel. He was going to remind her of the effect his lovemaking had on her—probably to demonstrate it. And she couldn't stand it—not now, wearing only her swimsuit and with him looking like he did. 'I'm going inside—to change,' she said indistinctly, and headed for the house.

Dirk was beside her instantly, putting his arm roughly round her waist and pulling her close to him.

'Into the dress you've been so busy mending?' he mocked, looking down into her eyes.

'Yes, if—if you like,' she breathed, intoxicated by the male smell of him, even the dust, even his sweatiness—wondering at herself because she should hate him to be near her, she'd always been a fastidious girl. And yet—oh God—fires of excitement raced along her veins and it was only with an effort of will that she prevented herself from lifting her face to invite his kiss. 'Please—let me go,' she said faintly, and then she felt her bosom crushed against the dustiness of his shirt, and the strong steady beat of his heart seemed to throb through her own body.

'Frankly, I don't care what you wear,' he muttered, his lips warm on her hair. 'You're a provocation in anything—or in nothing.'

She pulled herself away from him with a fierce little movement, and this time he let her escape and she ran panting through the garden to the verandah.

CHAPTER SEVEN

AFTER dinner that night, Dirk disappeared to the office leaving Matty and Patrick to play Canasta. Matty was shattered but determined not to show it. She'd taken it for granted he'd want to get her to himself tonight— make love to her. And though she'd told herself she was going to avoid an encounter with him, now that he'd walked out on her, she admitted she'd been stimulated by the thought of sparring with him. She was wearing her black and tan dress, but Dirk hadn't remarked on it at dinner, and that had piqued Matty too. She was, in fact, feeling really uptight.

Now sitting opposite Patrick at the card table, she couldn't concentrate on the game. Her thoughts, whether she liked it or not, went continually to Dirk and the uneasy situation she'd got herself into with him—a situation that was rapidly getting out of hand. It was as though she were hopelessly lost in some kind of emotional labyrinth.

She started when Patrick suddenly swept the cards into a pile, then sat back in his chair and looked across at her with brooding accusation.

'What's the matter?' she asked, falsely bright. 'Did I do something terribly wrong?'

'You haven't done anything for the past several minutes,' he said. 'Your mind's not on it, and I'm bored stiff too. What are you thinking about? My brother?'

Matty flushed, and as if that were answer enough he leaned forward and reached across the table for one of her hands.

'If you're besotted by him—and by Moonak—you're a fool, Matty. You'll never get as far as being the boss's wife. Dirk doesn't mean to marry you.'

Matty's brows lifted slightly. She knew differently. Dirk certainly did mean to marry her, but she was not, as Patrick put it, besotted either by him or by Moonak —or by the thought of becoming the boss's wife. She said coolly, 'What would you know about it?'

'More than you, at a rough guess.' She had pulled her hand away from him, but he stayed leaning forward, staring into her face. 'You're a pretty girl, Matty, and I'm the first to admit it would be a pleasure to make love to you. But don't kid yourself Dirk's likely to do anything more than just that. He's a very tough nut to crack, and to put it plainly, his one and only object is to stop me getting into bed with you first. He calculates a little sex starvation will send me haring off back to Lyndal—and after that it will be a short step to the accountancy firm, marriage, and living happily ever after. In Perth, of course, which is the whole meaning of this exercise. You're just what's known as a pawn in the game—you don't matter one little bit.'

A pulse had begun to beat at Matty's temple. How dared Patrick talk to her like that—judge her on one thing she had done years ago—assume she was the kind of girl to be played with, *used* like that. As if—as if any man who chose could get into bed with her. And the fact was, Dirk did mean to marry her, though why she didn't really know. *She* was the one who was holding off. But it was no use losing her temper and her dignity, so she clenched her fists and told him with icy self-control, 'I'm not interested in what you think of me and my engagement to Dirk. As it happens you don't know what you're talking about, and you're certainly overrating your own importance in the scheme of things. I know Dirk thinks you should make it up with Lyndal and marry her—and frankly so do I. After all, you've been sleeping with her for some time, haven't you?'

'I can guess who told you that,' Patrick exclaimed. 'And I can guess why too, but your sanctimoniousness doesn't impress me. If sleeping with a girl means you should marry her, then believe me, my brother ought to have been married several times over by now ... Has he got you to bed with him yet? When you were a school-girl you used to be rather eager about that kind of thing, I seem to recall.'

Matty went white. By now she knew all too well what he thought of her, yet what could she say? Would it do any good to protest innocence? Wouldn't Patrick simply laugh at her? She'd done a stupid thing four years ago, and she couldn't forget she'd told him no one cared if she stayed out all night. She was unhappily aware too that it hadn't been her fault her virtue had been left intact, and the thought made her feel sick. She'd learned a lesson then, and though she hadn't learned it in the hardest way of all, it had stuck. Yet now, when it came to going to bed with Dirk, what use was that lesson to her? In her heart she knew it could quite easily have happened by now—if Dirk had chosen to have it happen. The fact was, she——

Suddenly she drew back from her too revealing thoughts. Ignoring Patrick, she got up from her chair and walk distractedly out of the room and on to the verandah. There she leaned against the rail and stared into the dark garden, her heart beating fast. Patrick's crudeness had hurt and humiliated her, but that wasn't what bothered her just now. It was the frightening dis-covery she'd inadvertently made.

She'd fallen in love with Dirk. That was why she would consent if he chose to make love to her.

She put a hand to her breast and pressed it there. She felt agonised. She wanted Dirk with her now—she wanted him so badly she didn't think she could bear it. She wanted his arms around her, she wanted to lay her head on his breast, to put her lips to his bare skin, to

let her tears flow there. She wanted to be comforted—
to have him tell her that he loved her—that that was
why he wanted her to marry him.

In the darkness she heard herself utter a brief broken
laugh that was half a sob. Matilda Segal was losing her
senses—trying to cast a hard cynical man like Dirk
Reasoner in that kind of role. Why couldn't she be
satisfied with the fact that he was actually willing to
marry her, and go along with that? Stop fighting, just—
let it happen ...

It was easy enough alone in the darkness of the night to
think that way, but by morning Matty was irresolute.
In fact, she'd reached the conclusion as she dressed
quickly before breakfast that she'd let her imagination
run away with her. She couldn't possibly just go along
with Dirk's demand that she marry him. Tomorrow,
when they went to Ridge Creek, she'd do exactly as
she'd planned. The sensible thing. The only thing. She
wouldn't come back. That would at least put the ball
in his court, she told herself wryly and even a little
tragically, as she zipped up her black jeans and pushed
her feet into sandals.

Dirk and Patrick were at breakfast on the end of the
verandah when she made her way there, and she knew
from the surge of hot air that swept in from the garden
that another sizzling day was coming up. She was full
of nerves as she took the chair Dirk pulled out for her
and said a rather subdued good morning to the two
men. They greeted her, then went on talking as she
helped herself to tea and buttered a slice of toast, which
she nibbled at without much appetite. She had been
aware of Patrick's half hostile look when she joined
them, and their conversation of last night came back
unpleasantly into her mind. Patrick owed her an
apology, to her way of looking at things. Whether she

owed him one too she was not sure. What should a house guest do in these circumstances?

Try to forget it, Matty told herself, sipping the hot tea. Just be polite and pretend nothing's happened—you haven't been—insulted. Maybe Patrick hadn't seen it that way anyhow, and she suspected he might be more cut up than he made out about the break with Lyndal. Add to that the fact that Dirk didn't want him at Moonak, and it would seem he must be having quite a bad time just now. Perhaps that was some excuse for his rudeness.

Her eyes went to Dirk, and immediately a feeling of weakness overcame her. She studied him through her lashes—that strong handsome face, with its touch of savagery, of ugliness. His nose was very slightly crooked and no amount of shaving could make his jaw anything but dark. Did she really think she was in love with him? She heard her own indrawn breath as the inescapable answer struck her, and Dirk looked at her briefly. She became more conscious of the conversation, which had she had been vaguely aware concerned what they had been doing the previous day. Apparently this morning they were going out on horseback to look for any straying cattle that had escaped them yesterday.

'I don't see the point,' Patrick was saying aggressively. 'The stockmen can do all that when the races are over. Besides, it's not much fun for Matty to be left on her own again, is it?'

'Matty can come along too if she wants,' Dirk said unequivocally. 'And you can quit arguing, Patrick, and keep in mind the fact that I'm the boss and you're the jackeroo. You wouldn't last five minutes anywhere else with your attitude ... You can drive out to the western paddock this afternoon and check the fences there. You'll probably be late back, so get Ruth to pack you up some tucker.'

'Tremendous,' Patrick muttered, as Dirk wiped his

mouth on his table napkin and with a murmured excuse got up and left the table.

Neither Matty nor Patrick said anything to each other as they finished their meal, and it was only out of politeness that Matty sat there till Patrick drank the last of his tea.

She was tidying her room when Dirk came in—without knocking and without announcing himself. He sat down on the chair by the mirror and started rolling a cigarette before he'd even said a word.

Matty, who was finishing making her bed, felt her heart begin a nervous tattoo. It was on the tip of her tongue to demand, 'Who gave you permission to come into my room?' but for some reason she said nothing, but acted as though he weren't there.

'What did you and Patrick get up to last night?' he asked, after several minutes had passed, and Matty turned and looked at him across the room, somewhat taken aback. He licked the cigarette paper and looked back at her, his dark eyes expressionless.

'Nothing,' she said. 'I don't know what you mean.'

'Thunder in the air,' he said briefly. 'Did he make a pass at you?'

'No.' She had coloured, annoyingly. 'He was just warning me against you.'

'What the hell are you talking about?'

'Patrick says you don't mean to marry me, that's all,' she said. 'He—he thinks I'm making a fool of myself.' Once it was said, she wasn't sure if she should have told him, and she preferred not to remember the feelings that had almost overcome her on the verandah last night. She found it distinctly unsettling to have him sitting here in her room, and now that her bed was made she didn't know what to do with herself. Behind him in the mirror she caught a glimpse of her reflection —a brown-haired girl, her hips rather skinny in the tight black jeans, though her bosom showed rounded and curved through the fitted shirt she wore—one of the expensive sort she'd grown used to buying for herself in Perth, and that she'd have to learn to live without in the near future, she reminded herself realistically.

Dirk was smiling at her crookedly.

'Oh, I mean to marry you, darling,' he said. 'You know that.'

He'd called her darling in exactly that careless way before, but this morning it did something quite drastic to her. It sent a shiver all along her nerves, and she watched him almost fearfully as he got leisurely to his feet, so that suddenly the whole room seemed filled with his personality. In black trousers and brown and black checked shirt, he looked bigger and tougher than ever, and though his appearance was immaculate just now, Matty was aware that before this burning hot day was over he'd be dust- and sweat-stained. And she knew too that she was absolutely crazily in love with him.

Meanwhile he was looking at her from narrowed eyes, a half-smile on his long enigmatic mouth.

'Anyhow, are you coming out with us this morning?'

'Not if I'll be in the way,' she said awkwardly. 'I mean, if you're going to work the cattle——'

'We're not exactly going to do that, and you won't be in the way. You're a good horsewoman, and you're not entirely ignorant of stockwork in any case, I imagine. You must have seen what went on at Glenna Downs.'

'Yes, but I was only a child then,' said Matty, unnerved by the very mention of Glenna Downs. She wished that Jerry had never told Dirk about her father's property.

'You don't easily forget things you learn as a kid,' Dirk said. 'You'll be all right—we'll only be dealing with a few straying beasts, if that ... Finish getting yourself ready and I'll see to the horses.' At the door he turned back to say, 'You made a neat job of mending your dress, by the way.' And then he was gone.

Why on earth should a simple little remark tossed off like that actually make her feel a glow? 'Matilda Segal, you're a hopeless idiot,' Matty told herself.

They rode a long way that morning, and though it was hot and the flies were bothersome, Matty derived immense pleasure from her visual impressions. Looking across the lightly timbered flats towards the long low hills was like contemplating some perfect and unreal pictures from a remote dreamtime. Groves of trees showed dark against the pallor of the long dry grasses, and there were splashes of red and purple from the termite mounds. Some of these were miraculously fluted, some were like ancient, weatherworn sculptures of squat deities that looked more Chinese than aboriginal, and of course were neither. There was a hint of crystalline purple in the air—something she had noticed before, and that made her spine tingle with delight, it was so delicately dramatic, so remote, yet so—immediate, it seemed to impose its quality on one's own life.

She wanted to tell Dirk something of the way she felt, though she knew it was inexpressible, but all she dared do was look into his face and try to read there if he too was affected by all this strange and primitive beauty. But his face was impassive, his eyes narrowed, the line of his mouth enigmatic.

No, she had no idea what went on in his mind, and he didn't even turn his head to look across at her, riding fairly close beside him. He was intent, she supposed, on the work he had set for himself and Patrick.

As for Patrick—she was vaguely aware that he was having a little trouble with his horse. He was riding some way behind, but even so she heard him say viciously, 'You brute of an animal! Don't try your wits against me!'

If Dirk heard too he had made no sign, and Matty thought uneasily that Patrick was in a decidedly ill-humour. Perhaps not merely because he hadn't wanted to come out today, but also because of his broken affair with Lyndal. There was not a thing she could do about it, of course, and no real reason why she should want to, when she reflected on his rudeness to her. Yet later, when Dirk suddenly rode ahead, she waited for Patrick and told him a little stiffly, 'Patrick, I'm sorry we—quarrelled last night. I didn't mean to moralise about you and Lyndal, you know, but I felt it was pretty mean of you to—to suggest I was——'

She hesitated, and he finished for her, 'Hardly in a position to throw stones? Well, first impressions do stick. Anyhow, you go right ahead—have fun with my brother. But don't count on being a permanent fixture in his life, that's all.'

What was the use? Matty dug her knees into her chestnut's sides and raced ahead again. The fact was, she was in a very odd situation. As she couldn't sort it out herself she could hardly expect Patrick to understand.

At the edge of the open grassland they were crossing was a great stretch of scrub curving around from the left, and Matty saw that Dirk was going to search for stray cattle there. Presently he shouted back over his shoulder, 'There's some cattle in the scrub. I'm going to hunt them out. Keep them in the open, Patrick, and we'll sort them out.'

He rode on and Matty let her horse cover a few more yards before she reined in and waited for Patrick to come abreast of her.

'What was Dirk yelling about?' he asked cantankerously.

'Didn't you hear?'

'Would I be asking you if I had?'

Matty made a little grimace, then told him exactly what Dirk had said. Half her attention was on the tangled mulgas, with their fantastically twisted branches, and the mingled shadow and brilliant sunlight made her blink. Her chestnut was standing quietly, but Patrick's horse, a gelding, larger and more powerful, was fidgeting and edging sideways, its nostrils flaring nervously. A faint haze of dust was beginning to rise into the air over the trees, and Matty knew Dirk must have got some cattle moving.

'What can I do?' she asked Patrick quietly. She was aware her horse had been trained for stockwork, and she felt confident she could be of some use. But apparently Patrick had other ideas.

'How the hell should I know?' he snapped ill-humouredly. 'If you're likely to get in the way you'd better disappear.'

Matty bit her lip and looked around her unhappily. She wasn't sure if she should ride off to the far side of the scrub and wait in the shade there, or if she should just stay around and help in any way she saw fit. But as Patrick was so obviously not interested in having her assistance, perhaps she'd better do as he said, and disappear.

She was on the point of riding off when a bull erupted from the scrub and came lumbering towards them. It pulled up when it saw the horses, stood for a moment, its great head swinging from side to side, then turned and began to move briskly, though at a tangent, towards the trees.

'You won't get away with that,' thought Matty. She held her reins lightly, knowing her horse wouldn't move without her giving it a lead. She remembered watching the stockmen on Glenna Downs—and her own father—pursuing a runaway beast. The procedure was to catch up with it, gallop alongside, then wheel across and head it back to the mob or the stockyards or wherever. Patrick had the whole of the open plain at his disposal, so there should be no problem, and now she watched him spur his horse on and ride ahead of her. A minute later, for no reason that she could see, he brought his whip down cruelly on the gelding's flank. The horse propped, and Matty uttered a soundless gasp, expecting to see Patrick lose his seat and slide to the ground.

It didn't happen. He was still in the saddle as the horse came down again and galloped madly off—but instead of pursuing the bull it headed off in the opposite direction.

That horse of Patrick's was hopeless, she thought, and she wondered at Dirk allowing him to ride such a brute, and one so plainly useless when it came to stockwork. Though at any moment she expected Dirk to appear, she decided she'd better make an effort to stop the bull from escaping back to the sanctuary of the trees, and she pressed her knees into the chestnut's flanks and urged it to race forward.

The bull was blundering along fairly slowly now, but though Matty's horse flew over the ground like the wind, it had gained the trees before she caught up with it.

It was then she made a mistake.

She glanced back over her shoulder to see if Patrick was coming to the rescue, and an instant later she was almost swept from the saddle by a low-hanging branch that caught her a blow on the head. She gasped with pain and crouched low—too late—and pulled on the reins. Her horse stopped instantly and she was dabbing at her cheek and feeling a little dazed and quite badly shaken when Dirk rode through the trees towards her.

'My God!' he exclaimed. He swung down from the saddle and leaving his reins dangling came swiftly to her through streaks of sunlight that looked blindingly red to Matty.

'It's nothing,' she told him, trying to smile. 'I just got—mixed up with a branch.'

He reached up to her and somehow she was sliding down from the saddle into his arms.

'Where's Patrick?' he asked tersely, at the same time examining the damage that had been done to her face.

'His horse ran off—it's been playing up all the morning.'

He muttered something she couldn't hear, and lines of anger appeared beside his nostrils.

'We'd better get you home and attend to those scratches,' he said. 'There's a nasty gash under your eye —thank God it *missed* your eye and you're going to have a bruise on your forehead by the look of that swelling.'

'It's nothing,' Matty protested, though she was aware of the trickle of warm blood down her cheek and her head was beginning to throb. She looked around her vaguely. 'Where did the bull get to? I'm—I'm sorry I let it get away.'

'*You* let it get away? I didn't ask you to head it off— that was Patrick's job. What the hell was he thinking of to let you get mixed up in this?'

'It wasn't his fault,' she insisted. 'I told you, his horse was playing up. It's a—a cantankerous animal. Patrick nearly got thrown! It wasn't his fault I tried to take over or that I—I didn't look where I was going.'

Patrick came through the trees—on foot—as she spoke, and Dirk turned on him.

'What do you think you're up to, letting Matty try to do your work for you?' he demanded roughly. 'She's cut her face to ribbons while you've been fooling about doing God knows what.'

Patrick's face was streaming with perspiration and he looked slightly green, and Matty felt sorry for him. 'That horse should be shot,' he muttered. 'It's a horrible, vicious brute——'

'Oh, don't give me that stuff—it's a good camp horse.'

Dirk turned abruptly away from his brother. 'Are you feeling okay, Matty? Do you think you'll be able to ride home?'

'Yes, of course,' she said. She was troubled about Patrick. She'd seen the way his horse had behaved, and about to put her foot in the stirrup she paused and told Dirk determinedly, 'It *is* a brute of a horse, Dirk. I saw. I—I don't think you know——'

'I do know,' he interrupted, his voice harsh. 'I know all the horses presently in use on Moonak. What's bothering you? Do you think Patrick's going to be killed if he rides back to the homestead on Dallas?'

She met his eyes. 'No. But I think you're being unfair.'

'Then stop thinking and mind your own business.'

Matty turned away from him, her cheeks burning. She climbed into the saddle, took her reins from Dirk without looking at him, and turned her horse's head.

All the way back to the homestead, she and Dirk stayed in the lead, and Matty forced herself not to look back to see how Patrick was faring. She didn't quite know what to make of the incident, but she had the uncomfortable feeling that Dirk was deliberately making things hard for Patrick, and that she didn't like. Just because he didn't want him here——

The cuts on her face had begun to throb by now, and she was finding the burning hot sun almost too much to bear. She was exhausted when they finally reached the homestead and it was the greatest relief to go into the cool of the house. Matty went straight through to her bedroom where she was shocked by the sight of her face in the mirror. The cuts and scatches she had received looked even worse than they felt, and one of her lids was beginning to swell so that she looked really battered.

She was still staring at herself bemusedly when Dirk came to treat her wounds, bathing them with disin-

fectant and examining them minutely. She emerged
with plaster over the deepest cut—the one below her
eye—and ointment on the bruise on her forehead while
her various other scratches were to be allowed to heal
uncovered. When Dirk had gone, she changed out of
her jeans into a cotton dress, and rather shakily made
her way to the dining room for lunch—to discover that
she and Dirk were to eat alone. Patrick, it appeared,
had already gone out in the jeep to the western paddock to see to the fences.

'In this heat?' said Matty, and shuddered. She was
still feeling sorry for Patrick.

'You think me unjust, don't you?' Dirk remarked, his
expression sardonic.

'Yes, I do,' she said vehemently. 'Oh, I suppose
Patrick is—is only the jackeroo here, but—that horse
Dallas—surely if Patrick doesn't like it there are other
horses he could have had——'

Dirk shrugged. 'One horse is much the same as
another ... You'd better rest up this afternoon, Matty.
You're cracking hardy, but you've had a shock and you
look sick on it.'

'What are you going to do?' she asked rather
pointedly.

'I'll be around,' he said dryly. 'I'm the boss, you
know ...'

Matty slept that afternoon. When she got up she felt
terrible, and her face *looked* terrible. Her eyelid was
still swollen, and she surveyed herself despairingly. She
dreaded the thought of going in to Ridge Creek looking
like this.

Dinner was late, because they waited for Patrick who
didn't come in till after seven o'clock. He looked done
in as he sat down at the dinner table, and he didn't
raise a smile once. Nor did he engage in conversation
except to report to Dirk, rather tersely, what he had
done during the afternoon. One would never think

they were brothers—or half-brothers, Matty corrected herself mentally. He had been put very firmly in his place this morning, and now he was speaking as any jackeroo might to a not too accommodating boss. He vanished immediately after dinner—to take a shower and get to bed, he said, managing to imply that he was the only one who had been working.

After coffee, Matty encountered him in the hall, on his way to the shower.

'You've made a pretty mess of yourself, haven't you?' he commented, blocking her way. 'You look like someone's dragged you through a barbed wire fence—face first. I suppose you told Dirk I made you chase that damned bull across the paddock.'

'No, I didn't,' she retorted acidly. 'As a matter of fact I told him your horse had been playing up and it wasn't your fault.'

'Very kind of you,' he said with a surly look. 'The fact is you should have done as I said and kept out of the way. It was mainly you prancing around that made Dallas so nervous and unmanageable.'

Matty looked at him speechlessly. That was just not true! Dallas had been nervous all morning—and she hadn't been prancing around. It was on the tip of her tongue to tell him so, but instead she gave a slight shrug and continued on her way back to the sitting room.

Despite her afternoon sleep, she was not feeling up to much and she'd just as soon have gone straight to bed, yet she didn't want to forgo Dirk's company, even though she was self-conscious about her battered appearance. She found him sitting back in an armchair, absorbed in one of the innumerable books he had on cattle breeding, and Matty took a chair and turned the pages of the magazine she had brought from her room. She pretended to read, but was conscious only of his unnerving presence. When she looked up momentarily, he raised his head too.

'Matty——'

'Yes?' She met his eyes and tensed as his glance followed the lines of her bruised and scratched face. Defensively she raised a hand to shade her swollen eye, and he smiled slightly, his expression quizzical.

'I don't think you'd better go into Ridge Creek tomorrow. Not looking like that,' he said.

'But—but my uncle's expecting me,' she stammered.

'I daresay he is. But he's not going to like it much if you turn up looking as though I've been knocking you about. He may conclude I've beaten you into submission, and what he wants is for you to be—looked after, isn't it?'

She coloured and turned her face away. 'I can explain,' she said stiffly. 'I must go—I must see him.' She thought wildly of her plans for escaping—not coming back—and she very much suspected she was not going to get away with it.

'I'll invite your uncle here,' said Dirk after a moment. 'That would be a very plausible thing to do under the circumstances, don't you agree?' he finished mockingly.

Matty surveyed him uneasily through her lashes. Plausible. Their engagement was a fiasco. Why did he insist they carry it through to marriage? It was crazy—incomprehensible. How different it would be if they'd really fallen in love with each other. Or at least, if he'd fallen in love with her—because she, undoubtedly, had lost her head over him. Could Patrick possibly be right? Was he merely using Matty to get him back into line? If he was, then he was taking somewhat drastic measures.

'What's worrying you?' Dirk said into her thoughts. 'Or can I guess? You think your uncle's going to find our engagement suspect. Is that it?'

Well, wasn't their engagement suspect? Matty looked down at the magazine on her knee. 'I—I think it would be easier to convince him away from Moonak.'

'On the contrary,' Dirk said dryly, 'I'd find it infinitely easier to convince him if he were here. Actions usually speak louder than words ... However, you're not going to Ridge Creek, and that's final. We'll invite your uncle here for a few days, and I assure you I'll do my best to put on a good performance. I think you'll find him willing to be delighted, anyhow, and if he's surprised, it will be pleasantly. I know he originally had my brother in mind for you, but in several ways I'm a better catch than Patrick.' He paused to smile ruefully, then resumed, 'As for our unseemly haste—it's not as if we were living somewhere where we could see each other constantly over a period of weeks or even months before jumping in boots and all. It's a case of now or never—sink or swim—in this remote part of the world.'

Matty looked at him helplessly. Why did he want to marry her? Was he protecting Patrick? And did he realise how she was beginning to feel about him? Because right at this moment, with him looking at her the way he was, her bones were turning to water.

Just then he screwed up one eye, got up and came to look down at her, his expression suddenly so clinical and impersonal that with a shock she remembered her unsightly face. He put out a hand to her.

'Let me look at those nasty scratches of yours and see if the healing process has begun.'

Embarrassed, she allowed him to pull her to her feet and draw her over to the light. She didn't look at him as he examined her face, and she felt herself tremble when he put one finger under her chin to raise it.

'You're a healthy young woman, Matty,' he said softly. 'You'll be as beautiful as ever in no time at all.'

He still had hold of her hand as he spoke, and he drew it against his breast. Unnerved, she looked up into his eyes. At once her heartbeats quickened and the blood ran through her veins in a race of excitement. She knew she wanted something more from him—to feel his body against her own, to be pulled into one of those close and sexy embraces that drew such wild responses from her. Instead, with her hand still in his he said almost abruptly, 'We'll make plans for our wedding—set a definite date—while your uncle's here. I'm not interested in long engagements. Are you?'

Matty's mouth felt dry and her senses spun. Stammeringly, and more to hide the truth from herself than for any other reason, she told him, 'You—you know how I feel about our engagement, Dirk.'

'I know what you keep telling me, darling,' he said. 'But your body tells me a different story. I'm prepared to give you no more than a couple of weeks to adjust, anyhow. Your beauty will be well restored by then—you'll be quite fit to be a bride.'

Two weeks! Matty nearly had a fit. In two weeks he expected her to—to promise to love, honour and obey till death—— The crazy thing was that she longed to do it, even though she knew the whole thing was impossibly unrealistic.

He let her go after that, and disconcertingly went back to his reading. Thus ignored, she felt utterly deflated. Obviously she was the only one in a fever. It seemed he could turn on the passion at will. It wasn't that Matty Segal in particular excited him. How could she just now, anyhow, when she was looking so frightful?

For a quarter of an hour or so she sat staring at her magazine and trying to sort out her feelings. And then, with a murmured goodnight, she went to bed.

CHAPTER EIGHT

SHE looked a little better by morning. The swelling round her eye had disappeared, but all the same she abandoned any idea she might have had of insisting on going to Ridge Creek. It would be too embarrassing to face the innumerable people who knew her at least by sight looking like this. Lance and Rona Fitzroy—all the people she'd met at Bunda Bunda—— No, it was impossible. She'd have a day to herself.

An empty day, she caught herself thinking, with Dirk not here.

However, over breakfast Dirk revealed that he wasn't going in to Ridge Creek either.

'You'd better write a note to your uncle,' he told Matty. 'Patrick can take it in.'

Patrick looked across at Matty with cold indifferent eyes, and once again she felt sorry for him. Things weren't going too well in his world lately.

'What shall I tell Jerry?' she asked Dirk. 'Do you— do you mean about getting my face scratched?'

'Of course I don't. You'll tell him about our engagement. And you can add that invitation we discussed last night.'

'Very well,' Matty said slowly, and leaving the two men she went to the sanctuary of her room, found pen and paper, and sat staring at the empty sheet for several minutes.

Everything that had happened at Moonak seemed so unreal, so unlikely. It was impossible to commit it to paper. True, she had come to Moonak to please Jerry. She had thought, upset as she was by what he had told her about his health and his feelings of guilt, that she would at least make an effort to set his mind at rest about her future. But had she, honestly, ever really believed she'd actually get engaged? She was quite sure she hadn't.

Yet here she was engaged to Dirk Reasoner of Moonak Station!—the least likely person in the world for her ever to have got tied up with. Most incredible of all was the fact that she had fallen in love with him.

'Dear Jerry,' she wrote presently. 'I'm sorry not to be able to see you in Ridge Creek today. I had a slight accident when riding yesterday. But don't worry, I didn't fall, I just scratched my face on some branches, and it's really nothing but vanity that's keeping me from coming to the races. Dirk would like you to come to Moonak for a few days because—you'll never guess, and I hope you'll be pleased—he's asked me to marry him. We haven't told anyone yet, of course, so keep it to yourself and we can talk it over while you're here.'

She paused to reread what she had written, trying to think how it would sound to Jerry, but before she could finish Patrick came into the room.

'I'll be leaving in a few minutes,' he said abruptly. 'Have you got the famous letter ready—telling all?'

'No, I haven't quite finished,' Matty said, flushing. 'I've asked my uncle not to say anything about—about Dirk and me, by the way, so I hope you won't either.'

He smiled sardonically. 'I'll shut up. I'm glad you're taking some notice of what I said, I really am, Matty ... Do you want me to place any bets for you?'

'No, thank you. I think I've had all the luck I can expect for a while,' she said, responding to his friendly gesture. 'Jerry drew Miss Fitz for me in the Calcutta at the hotel last Saturday, and I won five hundred dollars.'

Patrick's eyebrows went up. 'You did? Well, I've got news for you, Matty. Obviously you haven't got your money yet, because Jerry Bridle sold your draw to Malc Hardy for two hundred dollars.'

'What?' Matty didn't understand. 'How do you mean, he sold my draw?'

'He evidently didn't expect Miss Fitz to win, so to make sure you'd get something, he found someone else willing to take the risk—and stake two hundred on the chance of winning five. You'll get two hundred and that's all, Matty. It's not bad, but I guess money's not all that important to you anyhow, is it?'

Matty shrugged. Patrick believed she'd be coming into a lot of money in a little over a year, and while that thought made her uncomfortable she was worrying over what Jerry had done. He shouldn't have given her five hundred dollars, but she could guess why he'd done it. He felt so guilty about what he'd done with her investments.

She said abstractedly, 'I'll just finish this letter, Patrick, if you can wait a few minutes.' And to what she'd already written she added a few more lines. 'I know about you selling my horse in the Calcutta—I owe you three hundred dollars. Please don't think you have to do things like that, Jerry. I'd rather you were honest with me. Look after yourself, and I'll see you soon. Love, Matty.'

Once Patrick had gone, she felt uneasily aware that she was alone with Dirk. At one minute she hoped he'd be out all day, at the next she hoped he wouldn't. She was supposed to be marrying him in about two weeks' time, and the thought made her shiver. Some reckless side of her nature wanted to go on with it—to plunge in boots and all, as he had put it—to make it an accomplished fact. To have the right to sleep in his bed, to submit to his lovemaking, to—to revel in it. Could a woman feel that way about her lover when he was a lover only in the physical sense? Wouldn't there be a hunger for tenderness, for a closeness that went deeper than that? After all, what sort of a life could you build on a lopsided foundation like this? Lopsided in that there was love on only one side—hers; while on his, there was passion but no tenderness? Or was it a case of taming the tiger?

Matty didn't know that she really wanted to tame the tiger. She didn't want Dirk any different from what he was—fiercely male, earthy, domineering. So long as he would love her ...

Despite her tensed up feelings, he didn't take advantage of being alone with her, and the sense of anticlimax was somewhat devastating. At some time during the morning he went out in the jeep leaving her sitting on the verandah and not even bothering to ask if she wanted to come with him. When he'd be back she didn't know—except that it was sure to be before Patrick—and Jerry—were there. They probably wouldn't reach Moonak till very late at night. She wondered if Jerry would come in his own car. She didn't really think that a man in his state of health should drive long lonely distances on his own, and it was a relief to know that for the rest of the races up here he would at least have Jim Travers with him in case anything should happen.

The day seemed interminable. Dirk came back latish in the afternoon and the whole world seemed to change and suddenly become full of life and excitement. He greeted her, and then disappeared to take a shower. When he rejoined her he was shirtless, and wore only white pants that contrasted with the darkness of his skin. He leaned against the verandah rail and drank a couple of cans of beer, and leaning back in her chair she watched him though she pretended not to. He looked so clean and fresh, his dark hair gleaming and still wet. And all that expanse of bare body——

In her mind she could see her own fair skin against his darkness—she could imagine the strength of the arms that would hold her captive, the feel of his hands as they wakened her own passion to life——

'I'm going to take a swim in the pool when I've had this beer, Matty,' he said. 'I don't think you'd better come in—better keep those scratches dry at least today. But come outside with me, won't you, and keep me company. I'm sorry I had to leave you on your own today—there were a few things I wanted to see to.'

'Those cattle in the scrub?' she asked quickly.

'Yes. Only a couple of bulls as it happens, but they could ruin my breeding programme, and I prefer not to wait for the muster. We're going to be busy enough with other things then.'

'You—you won't really be able to spare the time to come to Perth,' said Matty.

His eyebrows peaked. 'Don't worry—I can get away when I want to. I have a good head stockman, and an overseer who lives at the south end of the run—a hundred and twenty kilometres away, in actual fact. But he can take over and they can carry on perfectly well without me. Mike's capable of taking the helicopter up, so there are no problems at all.' He straightened up from leaning on the rail. 'Well, are you coming out to watch me swim a few lengths?'

Contrarily, she wanted to say no, but she couldn't make herself do it. Of course she wanted to watch him swimming, she was hungry for the sight of him. As for their marriage—because that was the whole point of his taking her to Perth—she was beginning to believe it would happen. And, with a feeling of fate, she knew she was going to submit to it. She didn't really have much choice, she told herself. She'd have to go ahead—for Jerry's sake. Though that was an excuse that didn't really convince her any longer.

She watched Dirk swim—his head dark against the blue of the water—the powerful muscles of his back rippling. And she felt an inner thrill when he finally heaved himself out of the pool and came across the grass towards her, the water running off his body, his hips narrow in the black trunks that fitted like a second skin.

She suddenly thought of Rona Fitzroy who had laid claim to him, and again she wondered why he had chosen to marry Matty Segal, who was an unsophisticated twenty, and right now, with her lacerated face, a distinctly sorry sight.

She jumped up, suddenly unable to sit on the lounger as he came nearer, his eyes intently on her. She was wearing a long loose dress of fine cotton, nothing underneath it but the briefest of panties. The heat of the sun was going now, and a miraculously almost-cool breeze rustled through the palm leaves.

'When do you think they'll be here?' she asked Dirk nervily.

'Who?'

'Patrick and my uncle.'

'Not till tomorrow,' he said carelessly.

'Tomorrow!' she exclaimed, disconcerted. 'But I—I thought they'd be here tonight.'

'No. You're aware my brother likes to have a few drinks—but don't misinterpret that,' he added quickly. 'I'm not referring to the occasion you might think. It's just that lately there seems to be a perpetual crisis in his life ... He'll stay in town tonight and bring Jerry Bridle out in the morning. There's no point in using two cars, and besides, your uncle isn't familiar with the road.'

'No. I'm glad he won't be driving, anyhow,' she conceded. 'He shouldn't even be here, according to his doctor's advice.'

He looked at her darkly, his long mouth curved in a slight smile. 'If he'd adhered too strictly to doctor's orders, you and I wouldn't have met again, would we?'

Matty shook her head and looked away from him,

her colour deepening. The breeze caught her dress and moulded it against her body revealingly, and she turned away quickly.

'I'm going inside to change,' she told him, and fled.

That night after dinner, they sat outside in the comparative coolness of the dark garden. The house was still hot despite the fans whirring in the ceilings, and Dirk extinguished the lights and carried two cane loungers outside. A fantastic moon had drifted into a sky that still retained some of its coppery tinge, and the stars, big and hotly bright, hung low against the dark eternity of the heavens. Some night-flowering plant scented the air and the leaves stirred faintly.

Dirk rolled a cigarette and offered it to Matty, who shook her head, and for some time they leaned back in their loungers in silence, while Dirk smoked. From the bungalow beyond the trees, where the Cliffords lived, come the soft glow of light and an occasional drift of barely audible music.

'Would you like some music, Matty?' Dirk asked, his voice quiet and low in the darkness.

'I don't mind,' she said, though she didn't want him to move, didn't want the smooth surface of her mental pond ruffled. Yet it had already been disturbed merely by his speaking to her, saying her name.

'What's your choice in music? Pop?—disco?—the classics?'

'I'm mad about Beethoven,' she said.

'I have several Beethoven symphonies on record. Would you like to choose one?' She didn't answer straight away, and he asked bluntly, 'Or would you rather we talked? Frankly, I would.'

'What—what about?' she breathed.

'About ourselves, of course. We haven't talked a great deal, have we? Yet strangely, we've come to know each other pretty well.'

'Have we? I—I don't think we know each other very well.'

'I disagree,' he said lazily. 'At least, for my part, I've discovered a number of—quite vital things about you. Beginning perhaps with an awareness of your—distaste for Lance Fitzroy's attentions. To me, that was revealing. From a not entirely selfish viewpoint, I'm happy you didn't follow your early and rather wild ways. Of course, I know girls go on the pill when they're barely into their teens nowadays, and maybe it's a necessary precaution, modern morals being what they are, though I'll admit I don't like it. In my mind, morality—where it concerns sex at least—is a very individual matter that's tied up irretrievably with—well, with sincerity ... I suspect your morals have come a long way since you spent that night with my brother in Perth, and your aunt shrugged it off because you were on the pill.'

'But I wasn't! ' Matty interrupted fiercely. 'I—I was never on the pill. And no matter what you think, I—I didn't mean to—spend the night with Patrick. I only meant to spend an hour or two in your apartment before I went—home.'

'While he kissed you, I suppose.'

'Yes, I suppose so,' she agreed, a little exasperated. 'But isn't that perfectly natural? '

'Of course it is. And so is getting into bed and making love. And so is getting pregnant. I discovered that many years ago ... You haven't slept with a man yet, have you Matty?'

'No,' she said, relieved that at least he realised that. 'How do you know?'

'By the feel of you in my arms,' he said. 'By your reticences. By your trembling expectations. By your lack of guile and affectation. From a number of other more specific things too ... Anyhow, let's leave that subject for the moment. I was going to ask you about something else—about this private hotel where you work—doing the accounts, you said. You like figures, do you?'

'Not all that much,' she said with a shrug. 'But it was a way I could help Louise after Aunt Maisie died.'

'Louise! That unpleasant woman!' he exclaimed. 'Now why the hell should you want to help *her*? She didn't appear to care much about you.'

'No, but I—I lived there all those years after my mother died.'

'And paid well for the privilege, no doubt,' Dirk put in dryly. 'What sort of salary does she pay you for doing accounts, by the way?'

'Why, none,' she floundered. 'But I—I still live there, and you see, Maisie used to do it——'

'Well, *you're* not going to do it any more,' Dirk said tersely. 'You'll never go back there, so make up your mind to it.'

She shivered slightly at his tone—proprietorial, even —even protective. Yet she said defensively, 'I will go back, Dirk. I—I couldn't just walk out on anyone.'

'I hope that includes me,' he said. 'At all events, you'll go back to collect your belongings and to bring her up to date on what's been happening in your life, and that's all. Don't let your heartstrings be plucked at either, Matty. Beware of pity, in fact. Believe me, people like your aunt manage. She'll soon find someone else to do what she wants, and on her own terms too. But that's enough of that, if you find it controversial.'

They talked a little while longer—this time about Moonak—then Dirk went inside to fetch cool drinks—fresh lemon squash and a bottle of gin. Matty refused gin in hers, preferring the cool clean taste of the lemon.

After that, she thought it prudent to excuse herself and go to bed. There was an element of danger in being so alone with him.

Even so, her feelings were confused when he let her go quite casually, and stayed outside while she went into the house. It was still distinctly warm inside though Matty found her bedroom pleasant enough, so long as the doors and windows were open to let the cooler night air flow through. She undressed without putting on the light, then wearing a thin wrap-around cotton gown, she went to the bathroom and took a tepid shower. Back in her bedroom, she switched on the lamp that stood on the dressing table, and stood looking around her, seeing everything with new eyes. The rose-sprigged curtains, the two pretty twin beds, one on each side of the room. The very feminine chair in front of the dressing table, her own discarded clothes on the small armchair. She felt herself half guest, half very much at home, and she recalled vividly the night she had arrived here, and thought how much had been crammed into the few intervening days and nights since Dirk had pushed her down on the bed, unbuttoned her blouse—'Matty Segal,' he had said, 'will you marry me?'

She shivered inwardly and then she looked up to find Dirk standing in the doorway, still wearing the light-coloured pants that were all he had had on when they were outside on the loungers. Her heart seemed to leap into her mouth and for a long moment they stared at each other in silence. She had the strange feeling that the scene she had been envisaging was somehow there for him to see too, and her eyes moved compulsively down from his dark face, over his tanned chest to the leanness of his hips, and she heard her own indrawn breath.

She said, the banality of her voice and her words shocking her, 'I'm sorry, I—I didn't say goodnight to you properly before I came in.'

He smiled crookedly and then came into the room and put his hands firmly and possessively on her upper arms.

'Are you talking off the top of your head, darling? Or what do you mean by that remark?'

'What—remark?'

'About not saying goodnight to me properly.'

'I—I just meant it was rather rude to—to disappear.'

'I knew you hadn't gone far,' he said dryly. 'But how *do* we say goodnight properly, Matty Segal? Seeing we're engaged—and going to be married very soon.'

She raised her face nervously. Of course she wanted him to kiss her. But she couldn't tell him so, and she knew it could be inviting trouble anyhow. Dirk kept his hands on her shoulders, then lowered his face to hers and kissed her lips briefly and softly.

'How will that do?' he said mockingly.

Her eyes fell before his. It occurred to her fleetingly that his unusual gentleness might be out of consideration for her scratched face, and she felt a wild sort of despair. She told him with an uncertain smile, 'My face isn't sore, you know.'

His eyes travelled quickly over her cheek and brow, and glancing up, she saw something new appear in them—the hot fire of desire. At that moment she became aware that she wore nothing at all under her light gown, even though at the moment it was belted decorously.

'Goodnight, Dirk,' she said huskily, and attempted to step away from him. Instantly his grip on her tightened.

'A kiss on the cheek, a pat on the rump—and we part for the night,' he said. 'Is that your proper goodnight? Is that how you see it, Matty? Is that how you want it?'

It wasn't how she saw it and it wasn't how she wanted it, and she didn't resist when with slow deliberate fingers he unfastened her belt and slid the loose gown from her shoulders, letting it fall to the floor.

'You're as lovely as I remembered you,' he said unsmilingly, and she felt the blood surge hotly up and over her throat and into her face. Although she was frightened of what would happen next, she submitted unresistingly when he pulled her down on the bed beside him and gathering her to him embracingly, kissed her on the mouth. Soon his lips sought her breast, and his hands moved down her bare back, urging her against him so that her hips curved in to his.

What was going to happen? And was she—was she going to let it happen?

Through her mind flashed something he had said about sexual morality—about its being a very individual matter, tied up with sincerity. Suddenly she knew what it all meant. It meant you'd feel no guilt about letting a man make love to you provided you really loved him. And she loved Dirk—desperately. So much she'd—she'd die if she had to go away—never see him again——

'Do you want me to make love to you, Matty?' he murmured against her mouth.

She did—she did—and yet she couldn't tell him so. That would be to confess everything, and it was too much to ask. What did love mean to a man like Dirk— a hard, masculine, virile man? He wanted to marry her, of course—she knew that. And she knew too that he wasn't cruel in his passion. She'd learned that from her slight experience of him. Not cruel, nor vicious, nor disrespectful of her body. As for her—he had begun to fill her mind obsessively. She was crazy about him. If only he were crazy about her! Or—or was he? Did the hot look in his eyes mean that? Did his—consideration of her confirm it? Or was she fooling herself about his consideration? Because he'd made no attempt to woo her. Once she'd said she'd marry him, he had allowed her no second thoughts, he'd completely disregarded her protests that she didn't really want to marry him——

Meanwhile she hadn't answered his question, but regardless of that he was making relentless love to her, his lips, the touch of his hands, stirring her body with an unerring sureness, so that her most secret nerves were alive with expectation. She lay passive against him, and then instinctively she put her mouth to his shoulder and with her tongue tasted the salt of his skin —and closed her eyes and drifted halfway to heaven ...

When at last he moved away from her to sit on the edge of the bed and look down at her with dark sexy eyes, she experienced her first thrust of uncertainty. He was going to take off the one garment he was wearing— his light cotton pants. Then there'd be nothing to hold them back from each other. It was a tremendous, frightening step to take, to Matty's mind. They were going to be married, but—she hadn't thought about it enough, she didn't quite believe in it all——

Alarmed, she raised herself on one elbow and their eyes met for a long watchful moment. Then he laid a hand on her naked thigh and said unexpectedly, 'There are more ways of making love than just one, Matty ... Have I given you some pleasure, taught you something new about yourself—and me?'

She felt her face flame and then grow pale. So he wasn't going to do what she had thought—possess her, take that final fatal step. The knowledge was both relief and disappointment. But mostly, just now, it was relief, and she felt a surge of gratitude towards him. She felt newly aware of her nakedness, not through cold, because the room was warm, but because the windows were wide and anyone could look into the room. Of course there wasn't likely to be anyone looking through the windows. Moonak homestead was empty of everyone except Matty Segal and Dirk Reasoner. The Cliffords were in their own bungalow, the stockmen were away for race week, Patrick and Jerry wouldn't be arriving till tomorrow.

Dirk, when she came to think about it, could have

done as he liked with her. Yet he had made love to her
gently, so gently that he could have made more love.
And despite her half-hearted fears, she knew very well
that if he had stepped out of his clothes and insisted on
taking full possession of her, she'd have felt nothing
but a drugged delight.

Her mind went back to the morning when she'd
wakened in his apartment in Perth with Patrick lying
asleep only inches away. And how her innocent adolescent mind had explored the sensations in her body
and found nothing. Now, though Dirk hadn't made
love to her in the full sense of the word—now she knew
her body was not the same. Right now there were
centres in her physical being that were wide awake and
full of hunger. Hunger for Dirk—for his body . . .

Yes, he'd taught her something new. Perhaps he'd
taught her a little too much.

She discovered her glance was locked with his and
that she was incapable of replying.

He stood up, his eyes inscrutable. 'When your uncle
comes, we'll finalise our marriage plans. Right?' He
paused and she nodded, as if in a trance. 'Goodnight,
darling. Sleep well,' he said, and with a faint smile he
was gone.

Sleep well! Matty was sure she had too much to think
about. She felt centuries old in experience.

She rolled off the bed when he had gone and stood
naked on the rug, her hand against her mouth. She
wanted more than anything in life to follow him to his
room, to wherever he was going—and beg him to make
love to her—to make her his now and for ever. Not to
leave her tonight.

Across the room the reflection of her pale body glim-
mered at her mockingly, and with a shock she saw the
red marks on her face. She thought she'd remember this
moment for ever as she stood poised—ready to give

chase, to abandon all dignity, to humble herself and make the greatest confession of all—that she loved a man who didn't love her.

But after all, she didn't run, she didn't follow him. She switched off the light and lay under the sheet in the darkness. Her dreams that night were erotic for the first time ever in her life. In her dreams she was almost Dirk's—almost but not quite, because she didn't yet know what it meant to share a full sexual experience with a man.

CHAPTER NINE

IT was almost midday when Patrick turned up the next day, and he came alone. Matty, who had been waiting on the verandah while Dirk fiddled with the radio that had suddenly gone on the blink, stared unbelievingly as he climbed out of the car.

After a momentary hesitation she went out to meet him.

'Where's Jerry?' she asked without pausing to greet him. 'Is he driving out himself? He was supposed to come with you.'

'He's not coming at all,' Patrick said shortly. 'He'd arranged to go out to the river to fish for barramundi today, and tomorrow he's flying down to Perth. So I believe.'

Matty stared at him perplexed. 'But—but why? Didn't you give him my letter? Doesn't he want to come to Moonak?'

Patrick shrugged. 'Don't ask me how his mind works. Of course I gave him your letter and as far as I could see he was as happy as a cat that's been promised a saucer of cream a day for the rest of its life.' They had begun to walk towards the house and he put his hand in his pocket and produced an envelope. 'Here's a letter for you anyhow—and he sent you a kiss. I'll deliver that in a moment, too,' he added with an almost angry smile.

'You needn't bother,' Matty said sharply. She couldn't understand Patrick, though she was sure he wasn't happy. But it wasn't because she was going to marry Dirk, she was positive about that. She could only conclude that it was because of Lyndal. On the verandah she paused to slit open her letter and he caught hold of her and kissed her, full on the mouth—a kiss that was both savage and practised and, to Matty, alien and hateful. In was a hard, taking kiss that had nothing to do with tenderness and sympathy, and she was deeply aware that Dirk, even at his most ruthless—even back in the beginning, at Bunda Bunda—had never kissed her this way. There had always been a fire there—something that warmed her one way or another. Something that was specifically for her. An illusion, perhaps, but that was how she felt. Whereas to Patrick she was more an object than a person. Obviously, it would be an entirely different matter when he kissed Lyndal.

He had let her go and Dirk had come on to the verandah and no doubt witnessed the kiss. But he merely gave Matty one quick assessing glance before he asked Patrick, 'Where's Jerry Bridle?'

Patrick repeated what he had told Matty while she unfolded Jerry's letter and stared at it unseeingly. She wanted to explain to Dirk that she hadn't invited Patrick's kiss—to tell him the stupid reason for it. Absurdly, she felt as if she had been unfaithful to him. What must he think?

With an effort she turned her mind to Jerry's letter, aware as she did so that Patrick had gone into the house but that Dirk was still there, watching her.

'. . . your wonderful news,' she read. 'I'm happy for you, Treasure—really happy. You deserve it all. But I won't come to Moonak and get involved in a lot of discussion. You know all there is to know, and you've forgiven me like the sweet girl you are. I don't owe explanations to anyone else. Besides, Jim and I had planned a fishing trip—something I've always meant to do when I was up this way, but never got around to. I shall never be up here again, you know, it's all over. I won't go on to Wanganup now you and Dirk are engaged and you're off my conscience. I'll go back to

Perth—by plane. I'll leave the car with Jim in Kurranulla. It's for you, Matty. Pick it up some time if you
want to, or have Jim sell it. It's little enough, but I've
nothing else to give you. I reckon I can just about settle
my remaining debts when I get to Perth, and that's all.
Thank God you'll have Dirk to look after you when
I'm gone—you won't have to suffer for my sins. Don't
worry about the win from Miss Fitz—that amount of
money's not going to alter anything in my life, and you
might be able to buy yourself some wedding finery
with it. Be happy, Matty, and stay as long as you like at
Moonak—don't worry about me. Your loving uncle,
Jerry.'

Matty finished reading the letter and stood staring
into space for a full minute. She had the feeling that
Jerry believed he was going to die very soon—almost
that he was wishing it on himself. His affairs must be
in a mess. And it was certain that there was nothing at
all left of the money from Glenna Downs. Tears came
into her eyes, but not for herself. She thought she un-
derstood why Jerry didn't want to come to Moonak. He
was ashamed of himself and his feelings, he wouldn't
want to lay himself open to discussions that might reveal what he preferred to hide.

'Your uncle's not well?' Dirk said into her thoughts.
'Is that it, Matty?'

Matty looked up and nodded, her vision blurred by
tears that she tried to blink away.

'Don't be upset. I can arrange to get away in a few
days, and I'll take you down to Perth to see him. He's
flying down tomorrow, Patrick says.'

'Yes.' She looked at him gratefully. 'I—I think I
should go down.' It was odd, but not so long ago she'd
have jumped at the chance of going to Perth—on her
own—and not coming back. Now she wanted Dirk with
her—and she wanted to come back.

'I'll most certainly come with you,' he said. 'And we've our wedding to arrange.'

Their wedding. Hers and Dirk's. What had happened last night surged back into Matty's mind in all its detail. 'I love him,' she thought. Perhaps, once they'd really made love, once they were married, she'd be able to tell him what she felt. She shivered involuntarily.

Over lunch, Patrick mentioned off-handedly that Lyndal Stevens had been at the races in Ridge Creek.

'That's news!' said Dirk, helping himself to more of the salad that the housekeeper had made. 'What's she doing up our way? I presume she came to see you.' Patrick didn't answer, and he went on, 'I hope you took the opportunity to make up your quarrel.'

'No fear,' said Patrick. 'We're through. I like to arrange my life my own way. Though as a matter of fact, Lyndal told me she'd live up here, if that was what I wanted.'

'Well? Isn't it what you want?' Dirk said, his voice cold.

'Sure it is,' Patrick said cynically. 'But it's not what Lyndal wants. Not on your life. Once we were married, she'd blackmail me and get me back to Perth. It's the family that's put her up to this.'

'I wouldn't think so,' said Dirk. 'I always had the impression that Lyndal was a strong enough character to run her own life.'

'And mine?' With the handle of his fork, Patrick drew a heart on the white linen tablecloth, then put two crossed lines through it. A couple of seconds later, without finishing his meal, he tossed down his table napkin and got up. 'What have you lined up for me to do this afternoon?'

'Nothing at all,' said Dirk. 'My suggestion is you go back to town and pick up Lyndal and bring her out to Moonak. Since she's come all this way for your sake, the least you can do is to be civilised and talk things over with her. It's not as if she were some cheap little hussy who's chasing you. She's been your wife in all but name for some time now.'

Matty moved uneasily as if to draw attention to the fact that she was still there, but neither Patrick nor Dirk spared her a glance, and after a moment she went on eating, swallowing with an effort, tasting nothing.

'I've seen her,' Patrick said doggedly. 'I've talked to her. I'm not persuaded. She doesn't understand the way I feel about Moonak. It's in my blood—I belong here.'

'Belong here? For God's sake!' Dirk exploded. 'Why don't you take a good hard look at yourself, just for a change? Moonak's not in your blood, and you'll never be so much as a cattleman's backside. Try facing up to a few facts, Patrick.'

'What facts?' Patrick demanded belligerently, and Matty more than half expected him to put up his fists. But he stood where he was, his hands resting on the back of his chair, his knuckles white.

'Oh, work it out for yourself,' Dirk said wearily. He pushed his plate aside. He too had obviously lost interest in eating. 'By some quirk of fate you've been endowed with the same ability to deal with figures as your stepfather. In that, you're damned lucky, so why not stop hanging on to the romantic dreams of your long-lost boyhood? The city's where you belong. Be adult. Go to Ridge Creek and pick up your girl. She's given in gracefully. Now it's up to you to be honest ... I tell you, if you don't work it out pretty soon. I wash my hands of you. I won't have you jackerooing here, in fact you can get out and mess up your life any way you please.'

They glared at each other while Matty sat white-faced, then abruptly Patrick turned and walked out of the room.

'Fool,' Dirk muttered beneath his breath. He looked

at Matty though she was by no means sure that he saw her. 'I'm damned if I'm going to humour him any longer.'

'But—what's it all about?' Matty quavered. 'If Lyndal says she'll live in the outback, why shouldn't they stay here? Patrick's always wanted to work on Moonak, and even if his father wasn't a cattleman, it doesn't mean he can't be.'

'Look, Matty,' said Dirk, his face still grim and forbidding, his straight black eyebrows drawn down over glittering dark eyes, 'my brother can't handle horses, and he can't handle cattle, and that's a fact. Basically, he's afraid—and they know it. You should be able to work it out for yourself—you saw him with Dallas. The thing is, he won't admit it—not even to himself. Rather than do so, he'd disappear—kill himself hunting crocodiles, lose himself in Malaysia or South America or God knows where. He feels his manhood is at stake, and all because of some adolescent daydream he's hung on to— something linked up with the unfortunate circumstances of his birth.'

Matty was listening wide-eyed, her mind working overtime, and suddenly she saw it all. Patrick cursing his horse, lashing at it with his whip. She'd thought he was in a foul temper because of his love affair. But he hadn't been able to control Dallas—that was why it had been left to her to try to head the bull away from the scrub. And it was why, afterwards, he'd even blamed her for his horse's behaviour. She felt appalled.

'Of course, he can't help his fear,' Dirk added moodily after a moment. 'He's not a coward, far from it. On the contrary, I've seen him stick in the saddle when a far better rider would have been thrown. He bluffs his way through—he uses the whip—and most of my stockmen think he's a rather wild young man. But a cattle station is definitely not his world. I've always considered it was up to him to realise it and opt out, but he's still bugged by some idea of being rejected unjustly by my father. I should never have taken him on here, I suppose—I should have made him work it out on someone else's property.'

He got up from his chair and walked restlessly the length of the room and back, then stopped and looked down at Matty ruefully. 'Anyhow, forget it. It's all going to be worked out some way or another one of these days.'

As it happened, it was worked out sooner than either of them expected ...

Later that afternoon, Matty decided her scratches had healed sufficiently well for her to swim in the homestead pool. It was some time before Dirk joined her there, and then it was to tell her, his jaw set, 'I've been down to the yards. Patrick's taken Dallas out.'

Matty, hanging on to the steps, her body submerged in the cool blue water, looked up, her eyes crinkled against the sun.

'But why?'

Dirk shrugged. 'Maybe to prove to himself that I'm wrong. Well, I meant what I said. I've a good mind to pay him off next week and if he's so set on the life he can get himself taken on as a jackeroo somewhere else. Or go back to Perth.' He dived cleanly into the water, and that was the last either of them had to say about Patrick. Matty swam slowly up and down, not attempting to compete with Dirk, who was a far stronger swimmer. She had very mixed feelings about the affair, and she felt herself as involved as if she were part of the family. More than ever she was sorry for Patrick. Surely he must know in his heart that he couldn't make it here, that he wasn't equal to Dirk—and yet he wouldn't give in. Poor Lyndal, she thought, and in a curious way she felt herself very fortunate.

Patrick hadn't come back when at last they left the water and went inside to shower and dress. Then, as

Matty emerged from her room, wearing a long loose cotton dress, she heard the sound of a motor and went through to the verandah, expecting Dirk to be there ahead of her. But he was nowhere to be seen, and from the station wagon that had pulled up on the drive three figures emerged.

Rona and Lance Fitzroy she recognised immediately, but the slim fair-haired girl with them she didn't know. The very sight of Rona, however, was enough to make her heart sink, and then begin to thud.

Rona came up the steps first, and looked at Matty with unfriendly eyes, her eyebrows rising at the sight of her scarred face.

'So you're hostessing already, are you?' she tossed off unpleasantly, and walking past her, flung herself down in a lounger as if she had every right. 'Where's Dirk?'

Matty didn't answer. Lance and the fair-haired girl had followed Rona, and now they paused. Lance said civilly enough, his expression as he looked at Matty rather different from his previous air of patronising appraisal, 'Hello, Matty. Where's everyone? This is Lyndal Stevens, by the way—she wanted to come out to see Patrick, so we offered to bring her ... Lyndal, this is Matty Segal, Dirk's fiancée.'

Matty's smile froze on her lips. Who'd told Lance that? She'd asked Jerry not to mention it and she felt more than a little upset. It explained, however, what Rona had meant by her sneering remark—Hostessing already.

She murmured a welcome and invited them in— Rona had needed no inviting.

'Dirk should be here in a minute—we've been swimming,' she offered, and added for Lyndal's benefit, 'Patrick went out for a ride. I expect he'll be back soon too, though.' She and Lyndal exchanged smiles, and though she was probably only about her own age, Matty thought she looked quite mature and responsible, and rather nice as well. She was just wondering whether she should carry her hostessing a little further and offer to make tea or fetch cold drinks, when Dirk came through the house to the verandah. His eyebrows rose at the sight of the visitors, but he greeted them genially.

'I thought I heard a car. Great to see you, Lyndal—I hope you're going to stay with us.'

'I'd like to, but it depends on Patrick,' Lyndal said ruefully, while Rona watched Dirk through half-closed eyes. He hadn't sat down, and now he remarked,

'About Patrick—I've just found out his horse has come home without him, and I rather think I'd better drive out and see what's happened.'

Matty looked at him questioningly. He seemed quite unconcerned, but if Dallas had come home riderless, didn't that mean—trouble of some sort? An accident?

'May I come with you, Dirk?' It was Lyndal speaking, and Matty was certain the same thought must have occurred to her even though she spoke calmly.

'Sure,' Dirk agreed. 'Will you come along too, Lance? If it's okay with you, we might take your station wagon, seeing it's at the ready. I suppose you don't happen to have a camp stretcher with you?'

'We've got a couple,' said Lance, who had got to his feet at once.

'Great. I don't want to be an alarmist, but it just might come in useful. Well, let's be on our way. It's my guess Patrick will have gone out towards the river—there's not much pleasure to be had galloping round the flats in this heat. We'll head that way anyhow, and utter a few cooees, and see what emerges.' Dirk moved towards the steps with the other two, then said over his shoulder, his voice somewhat dry, 'You can keep—my fiancée company, Rona. I hope we shan't be long.'

They had gone, and Matty was aware of the venomous look Rona shot at her, and she quailed inwardly.

She hated the thought of being left alone with Rona, but she had no choice, and if Patrick had had an accident then extra passengers in the station wagon would only be in the way.

'Would you like something to drink, Rona?' she asked after a moment. She said it politely and she smiled as she spoke, but there was no friendly response from the other girl. Rona, in fact, looked at her with open dislike, and pushed the fair hair back from her face.

'That can wait,' she said coldly. 'I want to talk to you. Sit down.'

It was like an order, and Matty didn't sit down. Rona had no right to speak to her like that, or to take over as if this were her home and Matty were an erring employee of some sort. Casually, she moved over to the rail, and leaned against it without saying a word. There was no doubt in her mind that Rona wanted to talk to her about her engagement to Dirk. But whether she liked it or not, it was an accomplished fact. Moreover —and Matty was surprised how at this moment it all seemed so straightforward, so cut and dried, so unalterable—she and Dirk were going to be married in two weeks' time, and there was not a thing Rona Fitzroy could do about it. Dirk wasn't her property, and he'd never asked her to be his wife, however much she would have wished it.

Meanwhile, Rona had turned unfriendly eyes on her and was examining her face disparagingly.

'What on earth's happened to you? Have you been fighting with someone?—one of the kitchen girls?' she asked rudely. 'You're certainly the kind of girl who gets into brawls, aren't you? The kind of girl who—slaps faces——'

'And you're the kind of girl who *gets* her face slapped, aren't you Rona?' Matty retorted sweetly, and had the satisfaction of seeing the other girl's look of fury.

'But what was it you wanted to talk to me about? I don't suppose it was the state of my face.'

'You're right. I don't care two hoots about the state of your face. In fact, it could be scratched to bits and I wouldn't shed a tear for you,' Rona said viciously. 'It's your engagement to Dirk I want to talk about, you little snake.'

Matty caught her lower lip between her teeth to bite back an angry exclamation. If Rona was descending to name-calling, she certainly didn't intend to join her, and with an effort she glanced out across the garden and spared a thought for Patrick.

'You know what this engagement is all about, I suppose,' Rona went on, her voice loud and harsh, and Matty looked at her in surprise. She hadn't the least idea what Rona was talking about, and she didn't really want to know, because it was bound to be unpleasant.

'If you say so,' she said lightly, her expression deliberately implying that she wasn't interested.

'Don't take that offhand tone with me,' Rona snapped. 'Obviously you *don't* know what it's all about, and I'm going to enlighten you.'

Matty said nothing. Her pulses had quickened nervously, and she had half a mind to turn her back and walk away. Yet she couldn't. She knew she had to hear what Rona was going to say.

'That slippery swindler of a relative of yours, Jerry Bridle, put it all round Ridge Creek yesterday that you and Dirk were engaged,' said Rona. She paused, and Matty waited. She'd realised Jerry must have done that, and while she resented deeply the other girl's insults, she wasn't going to be drawn. 'Just the same way,' Rona continued, examining her nails—long, pink and perfectly lacquered—'as he carefully put it round the district that you're an heiress.'

An heiress! Matty flinched. Oh God, had Jerry said

that about her? How could he have done such a thing? Her throat was dry with distaste. She knew he'd misled Dirk about Glenna Downs, but to let everyone believe she was an heiress when the truth was so utterly different—that was frightful. It was inexcusable—even if he'd done it, as no doubt he had, to help find her a husband.

'An heiress,' Rona repeated slowly and meaningfully. 'I wonder if you realise that quite a few of the cattle stations in the North-West have been having a bad time during the last few years. Low beef prices, transport problems, staff difficulties—— But of course you wouldn't have a clue. You're from the city. Still, some of the really big cattlemen have been employing barely half the number of hands they had not so long ago. Moonak,' she said, and paused significantly, 'Moonak can certainly do with an—injection of money. And that's why everyone in the North-West knows exactly why Dirk Reasoner snapped you up. Everyone but you, of course. It's got absolutely nothing to do with your fatal charm, I'm afraid,' she finished, looking amused.

Matty had listened to her with thudding heart, and for several seconds she seemed totally incapable of making sense of what Rona was telling her. Then the truth struck home and she saw—she knew what her engagement was all about, as Rona had put it, and her world seemed to collapse around her. She'd puzzled and puzzled over why Dirk wanted to marry her, and now Rona had explained it—and it made the most shattering sort of sense. Matty was an heiress. Her money could be used for Moonak.

Well, all the North-West might know why Dirk had snapped Matty up, but none of them, Dirk least of all, knew that she didn't have any money, that Jerry's boasting was false. That Matilda Segal, far from being an heiress, had exactly five hundred dollars and one second-hand car.

It was ludicrous, and Matty wanted to laugh. But still more, she wanted to cry.

Rona had taken out cigarettes, and Matty moved further along the verandah rail, away from the cloud of smoke that would doubtless soon be coming her way.

'I hope you're going to be satisfied with a husband who's only interested in your money,' said Rona, blowing smoke. 'And I hope your fortune's likely to live up to Dirk's expectations. If it doesn't—well, you won't have much going for you at all, will you? Speaking personally, I'd never guess you had more money than would butter a slice of bread.'

Matty said nothing. There was nothing she could say.

CHAPTER TEN

OVER another hour went by before the others came back to the homestead, and afterwards Matty didn't know how she'd got through it. How do you get through time when you have to go on acting more or less normally even though something absolutely shattering has happened in your life?

She had vague memories of going out to the kitchen and making tea, of carrying her tray out to the verandah and hearing Rona say high-handedly, 'For heaven's sake, I'm not interested in tea! Why didn't you ask me, before you messed about with all this paraphernalia? All I want is a nice cool lemon drink with lots of ice in it.'

Matty acted as if she didn't hear her, and though she expected Rona to go through to the kitchen and get what she wanted, she didn't do so. As in a dream, Matty poured two cups of tea, floated wafer-thin lemon slices on top, and put the sugar within Rona's reach.

It was a relief to hear the car coming back, and she left her chair and went down the steps, but paused half way, her mind swinging like a pendulum between Patrick and Dirk. She was anxious to know if Patrick was all right, yet she shrank from confronting Dirk again, knowing what she now knew. That his interest in her was purely mercenary, that his lovemaking had been calculated, deliberate. And *he* had talked about sexual morality and sincerity, she thought hazily.

Lance and Dirk were carrying Patrick from the station wagon on a narrow nylon stretcher, while Lyndal walked alongside. From the expression on her face Matty calculated that Patrick couldn't be all that badly hurt, and though he was lying with his eyes closed he didn't appear to be in great pain.

All the same, he had apparently broken his leg, and once he had been established in one of the spare bedrooms, Dirk went to the office to contact the air ambulance so he could be picked up and taken to the Inland Mission hospital. Leaving Lance and Rona on the verandah, Matty went inside—to see Patrick, she told them, but that was mostly an excuse to get away, to be by herself. Lyndal was keeping Patrick company, and after a few words of sympathy, Matty went to her bedroom. There she stood in the middle of the floor and tried to think clearly and rationally about what Rona had told her.

She couldn't marry Dirk now, of course. If she had really been an heiress, if Jerry hadn't gambled her money away, it would have been possible. As it was, she couldn't marry him under false pretences. She wasn't an heiress. In fact, she had nothing for Dirk but her body —and her love. And while he might find pleasure in her body, that wasn't what he was marrying her for—and it certainly wasn't for her love.

So what was she to do?

She covered her eyes with her hands and thought desperately.

The simplest thing would be to tell Dirk firmly that it was all over. But then there was Jerry to consider. He'd been so pleased about the engagement, and after all, his life was very nearly finished. For his sake, she'd have to keep up the pretence a while longer. Only those plans of Dirk's for their marriage to take place in two weeks' time—she'd have to take positive action to stop that.

Meanwhile, she couldn't stay on at Moonak. She thought of last night and winced inwardly. To have Dirk make love to her would be ecstasy, even if it was merely because he was a skilled and practised lover. Oh, she thought, despairingly, how humiliating it was to be the victim of one's own body and its hungers! Love! Jerry had been wrong when he said there was no magic in love. There was—but it was black magic and she was caught inextricably in its spell.

How did a man's mind work? How did Dirk see all this? Didn't sincerity in emotion apply to him too, or was it merely a standard he liked to impose on the female of the species? Obviously, as far as he was concerned, Moonak came first. Which meant that if he married Matty and afterwards discovered she had nothing——

She had resolved nothing when Dirk spoke her name and came into the room. She straightened guiltily and moved to the mirror to brush her hair.

'Matty, I wondered if you'd make us some tea——'

'Yes, of course,' she said quickly, and their eyes met in the mirror. He moved towards her, cupped his hands over her breasts, and her heart began to race. What was in his eyes she didn't know, but she felt a feverish sickness as she looked back at that hard brown face and experienced what the mere touch of his hands did to her. Oh God, in spite of everything she was wild about him, she'd—she'd die for him. She wished and wished that Rona had never opened her eyes for her. Ignorance was certainly bliss. Yet how long would the bliss last when after marrying her Dirk discovered he'd landed himself not with an heiress, but with a penniless and lovesick girl?

She put hands that were suddenly clammy over his, pulling them away from her so she could turn round and face him.

'What—what happened to Patrick?' she asked unsteadily.

'He was thrown. He thinks Dallas caught his foot in a hole. The horse fell and apparently rolled on him, so it could have been a whole lot worse. As it is, he's done himself no damage apart from breaking his leg. I pumped a dose of pain-killer into him before we loaded him on the stretcher to bring him home. It's a pretty bad break, I'm afraid.'

'Oh, I'm sorry,' Matty exclaimed. 'I didn't know it was so bad.'

'Well, don't be too sorry for him,' Dirk said dryly. 'You may think me hard, darling, but it could be the best thing to have happened, in the long run—Patrick's chance to abandon Moonak without losing face, and I hope he takes it. I've been threatening to throw him out, but it looks as though a higher power's got in first and saved me the trouble ... Anyhow, about that tea——'

Matty made the tea, and some time later the air ambulance came and Patrick was taken away to the Mission hospital. It was during this procedure that Matty found herself temporarily alone with Lance.

'So you're going to marry Dirk Reasoner,' he remarked. 'Surprise, surprise all round. Jerry Bridle was tickled pink, naturally enough—though he was looking pretty green by the end of the race meeting.'

Matty's thoughts swung abruptly away from herself and her troubles. 'What do you mean?'

'Oh, following his usual form he took a gamble on the last race. Accepted a mighty big bet, and was up for a tremendous handout when the horse came in first. Most of his profits must have gone right down the drain. It's a good thing you're a well-heeled property owner, isn't it?'

Matty was scarcely aware of what he was saying. Her heart had dived at what he'd said about Jerry—that he looked green. She wasn't nearly as sure as Lance that it was because of a bad day at the races, but then Lance didn't know what a sick man he was. She asked him anxiously, 'Did you see him this morning—before he went fishing for barramundi with Jim Travers?'

Lance looked at her in surprise. 'Didn't Rona tell you while you girls were gasbagging in our absence? They didn't go on that fishing trip—your uncle was feeling too crook. Jim drove him to Derby to take the plane to Perth.'

That brought Matty's preoccupation with herself to a complete end. Jerry must be really ill if he'd gone to Perth, and somehow she must go and join him. He might have cheated her, but he was still her uncle and she was fond of him. Something would have to be arranged.

The two Fitzroys and Lyndal were staying the night at Moonak. It was a mixed blessing, because though it meant Matty wouldn't be alone with Dirk, it also meant she had to bear with Rona's presence, and that was something she didn't do gladly. She also had to suffer Rona as an onlooker when she told Dirk she wanted to go to Perth—and why. From the spiteful look of satisfaction on the other girl's face, she knew Rona thought she was making an excuse to get away, now she knew how little she meant to Dirk. It was galling to Matty, but there was nothing she could do about it.

Dirk at any rate was helpful—and unsuspecting.

'I realise how you feel, Matty,' he said. 'And I'll tell you what we'll do. It's on the cards Patrick will be flown to hospital in Perth—probably tomorrow. With a bad break such as he's sustained, it's essential he should get the best treatment that's available. That means Lyndal will want to get back home too, so how will it do if I run the two of you over to Derby as soon as we know what's happening? I'll follow you the minute I get things organised here.' He smiled at her significantly, and she knew he was thinking of their wedding and she looked away from him. It was at least a relief that he wouldn't be coming with her, and in the few days she'd have alone, she'd work out something . . .

As Dirk had predicted, Patrick was flown to Perth.

Matty packed her things with the feeling that she was saying farewell to Moonak for ever, and the Fitzroys left the station in their car at the same time as she and Lyndal left with Dirk.

'When's the wedding to be?' Lance wanted to know, but he asked Matty out of Dirk's hearing, so she was able to tell him coolly, 'We haven't decided on a date yet.' She would never see Lance again either, she thought, so it didn't really matter what she told him. Rona didn't even say goodbye to her, but that was no loss.

At the small airport Dirk kissed her goodbye, and soon she and Lyndal were in the plane and Moonak and the North-West were rapidly being left behind. Matty felt inclined to shed a few tears, but instead she listened to Lyndal talking about Patrick—about his accident, about his future and hers.

'He's got tremendous courage,' she remarked at one stage. 'He'd actually started to drag himself along the ground when we found him. He was in terrible pain— it's a very bad break. Dirk told me he might never be able to ride again—not the way you have to ride with cattle, at least. You know, being in the saddle all day — He'll be really cut up if he has to work in Perth. But at least I know he loves me—I know from the things he said after Dirk gave him that pain-killer.'

Matty listened sympathetically, and after Lyndal had got it all off her chest, they didn't talk much, and Matty tried not to think about Dirk, but to make plans for her own future. She'd have to find work, of course. There was no point in going back to Peppertree Lodge. Louise had never paid her for her work there in money —because Matilda Segal was wealthy! She would have to stay there for a while, she supposed, because Jerry would be there, but she'd look for work on the quiet. Meanwhile, she had five hundred dollars to subsist on, and with care it would last her long enough. It was certainly going to be awkward when Dirk came, with his wedding plans. Perhaps she could appeal to his good nature—persuade him to keep up the pretence that they were going to be married—for Jerry's sake. But no amount of thinking about it could convince her it was going to be easy. Dirk wasn't the type of man to be persuaded into anything he didn't like.

In Perth, she and Lyndal parted. Lyndal was going home, and Matty took a taxi to Peppertree Lodge, where she received a chilly welcome from Louise. Jerry was in town. He didn't look well, and probably he was in a financial mess, Louise said, judging by the amount of time he'd been spending with his solicitor.

'He tells me you're engaged to be married,' she added, and looked from the marks on Matty's face to her ringless hand. 'When's the great day? Jerry seems to think you're going to be rushed to the altar immediately, I'm not altogether sure why.'

Matty forced herself to keep cool. Trust Louise to be nasty, but she wasn't going to tell her a thing, and she merely shrugged and made a vague remark about nothing having been settled yet.

As she started towards her room, Louise stopped her. 'Now wait a bit, Matty. Things have changed while you've been away. I suppose you can sleep in your old room tonight, but you'll have to make your own arrangements tomorrow. I have a permanent guest moving in in the afternoon, and I've already shifted your stuff to the store room ... Now don't look at me with those great reproachful eyes, I can't build my entire life around you. I've been managing quite well without you, and after all, you don't need to stay here now you're engaged.'

'No, of course not,' Matty agreed quietly. It seemed to be just one more problem, but Louise was quite right in what she said, and after all, this wasn't her home.

When Jerry came back late in the afternoon she was

shocked at how ill and grey he looked. For the first time she knew that the doctor's predictions must be true, and she knew as well that he couldn't have done himself any good by going to the North-West. He had done that only for her sake. It would be impossible to tell him now that she wasn't going to marry Dirk after all, but it was painful to hear him enthusing—even gloating—about her engagement.

'I can almost fool myself I did you a good turn when I did what I did, Matty,' he said absurdly. 'But you needn't have come down to Perth just yet, you know.'

'Oh, Dirk will be coming down soon too,' she reassured him, and tried hard to smile.

He was angry to know that Louise had let her room, but she told him calmly, 'You mustn't worry about me, Jerry. I'll find somewhere to stay. There's no problem.'

'Go to a hotel, Treasure,' he urged her. 'A good one —the best. That's what Dirk would expect you to do. You've got some money—spend it. I can rake up more if you need it.'

'I'll be fine,' Matty assured him with a confidence she didn't really feel. She had no intention of going to a good hotel, of course, all she wanted was somewhere cheap and clean.

'When's the wedding?' was Jerry's next question—a question she was becoming tired of parrying. But she told him brightly, 'We haven't really talked about that, Jerry. There's—there's no rush.'

'For me there is,' he said wryly. 'I'd like to see you married before I die.' His face twisted, and she knew it was hard for him to accept death.

'If—if you look after yourself,' she faltered. 'Keep away from work——' She broke off as she met his eyes and saw plainly in them that he knew he was finished. It was the first time she'd read such a thing in anyone's eyes, and it shocked her.

The next morning she found a cheap clean hotel and

booked in. It would do for the present, but she'd find something more economical when she had more time to look. She bought a sandwich for her lunch, and before she went back to Peppertree Lodge she did a little window shopping. It was strange looking at clothes in the shop windows and knowing that as from now she'd have to think very hard before she spent any money. She'd been spoiled before, no doubt thanks to Maisie, who thought everything was going as it should. Her mother would have been horrified at what had happened, but it had happened, and there was no way of changing it, so it must be accepted. This, Matty suspected, was going to be one of the hardest periods of her life. Beginning with Jerry's confession and going on to the dilemma she was in now with his illness, and this engagement of hers that was based on a false belief. How many years would it take her to get over it all? she wondered.

That night she had dinner with her uncle at the guest-house, then telephoned for a taxi to take her to her hotel. She was waiting in the front hall with Jerry when Dirk arrived at the open door.

Matty's heart seemed to leap out of her breast. She felt herself flush and then go pale. She'd never dreamed he'd be here so soon—she wasn't nearly ready for him. She hadn't decided exactly how she was going to deal with the situation. And she certainly wasn't ready for the effect it had on her merely to see him.

His dark eyes took in what was happening very quickly—her luggage, the fact that she was dressed to go out, Jerry hovering near, his face lined and grey.

He greeted them both before he asked, 'Where are you moving off to, Matty?'

'To a—a hotel,' she told him unsteadily. 'I—there's no room vacant here just now, so——'

'Which hotel?' he interrupted, and there was nothing for her to do but name it. He didn't look particularly surprised, and it was Jerry who said flusteredly, 'I don't know what she's thinking of, going to a third-rate hotel like that. There's no need for Matty to be money-paring——'

The way he said it made Matty squirm—as though she really were the heiress Dirk believed her to be, but would discover all too soon that she was not. She didn't know what to say, but Dirk cut in firmly, 'I'll cancel your booking, Matty. Now I'm here, you're to stay in my apartment.'

She gasped slightly. There was only one bedroom in Dirk's apartment and she couldn't possibly go there. 'No,' she protested, but he refused to listen.

'No arguments,' he said, and Jerry of course urged her on.

'It's a wonderful idea, Treasure.' He turned to Dirk. 'I'm delighted my niece is going to marry you—in fact, I couldn't be happier. Mind you, you're getting yourself a wonderful wife—Matty's a very sweet girl.'

'I know that,' said Dirk, and to Matty's ears it sounded like a polite and meaningless remark. If he'd said, I know Matty's money is going to come in very useful at Moonak, she'd have believed him, but he was hardly likely to say that. He added, 'We plan to marry very soon, by the way. I'm going to make the arrangements while I'm in Perth. Matty and I can talk it over in the morning. We must also go along to the jewellers' to look at rings, and perhaps we'll be able to see you in the afternoon. How does that sound?'

'Fine,' said Jerry with satisfaction. 'Fine. The sooner you marry the better, as far as I'm concerned. And without wanting to sound gloomy, I reckon you understand why. I'd—like to go to the wedding, you know.'

'I understand,' Dirk said quietly. He reached for the telephone on the small table in the hall, and while Matty stood by helplessly, he proceeded to ring her hotel and cancel her booking.

As he'd dismissed his taxi, they took the one Matty had ordered, and she went out to it with him and Jerry and listened nervily while he gave the address. This was definitely something she hadn't planned on happening, but she'd calculated without taking into consideration the fact that Dirk Reasoner was a very masterful kind of man. Why she'd ever imagined he'd let her get away with anything she didn't know, but there was one thing she was going to have her own way about, and that was their wedding. It wasn't going to take place. It couldn't. Even Dirk wouldn't want it to, once he knew the real facts about her finances, and she quailed at the knowledge that she'd probably have to tell him the truth if she was to have her way. She wouldn't be able to protect Jerry.

Meanwhile, it was unthinkable that she should spend even one night in Dirk's apartment, and as soon as the taxi was moving, she told him abruptly, 'I can't stay in your apartment, Dirk. I—I didn't want to make a fuss in front of Jerry, but please tell the driver to take me to the hotel. My uncle needn't know——'

In the half dark, she felt his eyes searching her face, and then he put a protective arm around her and told her, 'Don't worry, darling. You're going to be perfectly safe with me.'

Safe with him—alone in his flat! Matty didn't think so. She pulled away from him and leaned forward, determined to tell the driver herself where she wanted to go. But Dirk's hand was suddenly against her mouth and she was back in the seat where she'd been before— only this time he held her a lot closer. With a sense of panic, she knew there was nothing she could do. Whether she liked it or not, she was going to his flat.

It was strange to be back there again, she discovered not very much later.

While Dirk put her luggage in the bedroom, she stood in the living room looking around her bemusedly, thinking of the girl she had been four years ago, and of the dangerous situation she'd got herself into then. She remembered too her first—and most terrifying—sight of Dirk, and she wondered if even then, deep down, she'd been attracted to him even while she was telling herself she hated him. She had certainly never dreamed then that one day she would be his fiancée . . .

When he came back into the room, he'd removed his tie and undone the three top buttons of the cream shirt he was wearing. Matty's eyes went over him feverishly. She loved him—she wanted nothing more than to marry him. And at that moment he moved towards her, took her in his arms and kissed her. First her eyelids, then her mouth. And she gave herself up to it weakly, responding to his kiss as wild thoughts chased each other through her brain. If she could know his love-making just once more—have just a little more to re-member——

And a lot more to forget, she reminded herself, and sick with despair tore herself away from him.

'Dirk, I can't stay here,' she told him wildly. 'Please. Let me go to the hotel.'

'Calm down, darling,' he said, smiling a little. 'What's bothering you so much, anyhow? Surely at this stage you can't think I intend to seduce you and then skip off and leave you pregnant! Haven't I made it clear we're going to be married the minute it can be arranged?'

She shook her head confusedly, but when he tried to pull her back into his arms she stepped away from him quickly.

'You're upset about your uncle, is that it?' he said after a moment. 'But that's all the more reason for you to stay here—with someone who cares about you. Some-where you can get yourself a drink or a snack in the night, or have a talk if you feel that way. If it's the sleeping arrangements that are bothering you, forget it.

I'll sleep in here on the couch. We won't make love till we're married.'

'All right,' Matty said defeatedly. He was so persuasive, and it was weak of her perhaps, but just now it seemed the easiest thing to do. Tomorrow was soon enough to take a stand—tomorrow, when he started talking about rings, wedding dates. Tonight she would stay here, sleep in his bed—alone. Just tonight. After all, he promised he wouldn't make love to her ... She raised her face and told him exhaustedly, 'I'm tired. I'll go to bed now, if you don't mind.'

'Of course I don't mind, darling. Would you like a drop of brandy to help you sleep?'

She shook her head. 'I'll be all right, thank you, Dirk.' She moved to walk past him, but it wasn't going to be as easy as all that. He caught her to him with strong arms, but this time before he could kiss her, she turned her head aside. She mustn't give way to her weak desires—she must face up to the fact that she was never going to be his wife, that she had to learn to live without him.

'No goodnight kiss?' he said, his fingers tightening almost cruelly on her shoulders. 'Why not?'

'I—I don't feel like it,' she said, and with a desperate movement she twisted out of his grasp and half ran across the room to the bedroom.

Dirk had left the wall light burning, and she shut the door behind her and leaned against it, breathing quickly. Should she lock the door? She knew she'd made him angry, and she looked wildly around the room—at the double bed with the quilt already removed and the sheet turned back, at her suitcase on a cedar chest by the window. At Dirk's tie flung down on the dressing table. At the door that led into the bathroom. Her heart seemed to stop for a second. Of course she couldn't lock the door. Dirk would need to use the bathroom—and to do that, he had to come through the bedroom.

With a feeling of panic, she opened her suitcase, found her nightgown and her toilet things, and shut herself in the bathroom to get ready for bed. She'd have liked the comfort of a warm shower, but her main object was to get to bed as fast as she could so she could pretend to be asleep when Dirk came through.

She'd been in bed for some minutes when he knocked softly at the door. Matty didn't answer. She turned on her side and closed her eyes. She heard the door open, heard the soft sound of his footsteps as he crossed the room, the slight click as he shut the bathroom door. Her heart had been beating madly, but now it slowed down a little. All she need do was to lie still and breathe steadily as though she were asleep and she'd be safe until morning.

She heard the shower running, then it was turned off and there was silence for a while. Click. The bathroom door was opened. Matty lay rigid under the sheet. Eyes closed, she waited to hear him cross the room. Instead, his footsteps came nearer and nearer and then stopped.

'Matty?' he said.

She didn't answer. She concentrated on her breathing, but for some reason it didn't fool him. She heard him move, heard him switch on the bedside lamp, and knew he was standing by the bed looking at her.

'Matty?' he said again, and this time, she rolled over and opened her eyes and looked at him. And wished she hadn't. He wore off-white cotton trousers, his feet were bare and so was his chest, and he looked disturbingly male and handsome. She heard her own indrawn breath.

He asked abruptly, 'Why the coolness just now? Don't you trust me—after all this time?' Colour flooded her face and receded. She felt too confused to speak. 'Don't you know I love you?' he said.

Oh God! Her heart jumped and tears sprang to her eyes. She didn't believe him, of course—but they were the words she'd longed to hear. She blinked her tears back and stared at him uncomprehendingly, and saw his face soften strangely.

'Your uncle's right,' he said gently. 'You need someone to look after you. He'll be happy to see us married.'

Oh, if only she could marry him! But she couldn't—and she was going to have to tell him why. Why not now, instead of putting it off until tomorrow? She'd never sleep now, if she still had that ahead of her. And besides, who knew what was likely to happen tonight if she didn't tell him?

She sat up in the big bed and looked straight at him.

'Dirk, I have to tell you this. I'm not going to marry you. Not ever. I know Jerry would like it—I know—I know he has to die. I want him to be happy, but—I can't marry you. So please, if we could just let him believe——'

Her voice trailed off shakily. His mouth had hardened and an ugly look had come over his face so that she was conscious again of his slightly crooked nose. She saw a muscle move in his jaw and she dropped her lashes, her gaze sliding nervously down to the darkness of his chest, then back to his face again as he demanded, 'What the hell are you talking about now, Matty Segal?'

Quivering, she was totally incapable of answering him—not when he was looking at her like that.

'My God,' he muttered, 'when I have you in my arms, when I see the way you look at me—even now, at this minute, when I feel you trembling against my body—I know damned well you love me.' Again he paused, and still she couldn't speak but stared at him transfixed. 'So what's wrong? Come on, now—you'd better tell me the lot, because you're greatly mistaken if you think you can wriggle out of your promises without any explanations. Just get that very firmly into your head.'

Matty swallowed. The moment had come. She had to tell him——

'I know why—you want to marry me,' she said after a silence that seemed to last for ever. She was wishing her voice wouldn't shake—wishing she could find some way of saying it that didn't sound too awful—wishing she didn't have to say it at all, wishing most of all that Jerry had never gambled her money away, that she could give it all to Dirk—— 'It's because—it's for Moonak, isn't it? Because things are bad—you need—— And my uncle—everyone in the North-West has heard that I'm——' She stopped and swallowed again, and almost choked on the words. 'I'm an—heiress.'

Dirk's dark brows rose and his mouth curved, though it wasn't in a smile. He looked at her for perhaps ten seconds without saying a word, and Matty wished she could die.

Then he sat down on the edge of the bed. His eyes travelled slowly over her face, exploring, it seemed to her, the scratches that were beginning to dry, the bruises that were fading. They lingered on her trembling mouth, then moved to her bosom, its curve revealed by the clinging softness of her nightgown. Finally he said dryly, 'So you think I'm marrying you for your money. Is that it?'

Matty shivered inwardly. She lowered her lashes and hunched up her knees under the sheet. This was the weirdest situation—to be here in his bed, talking this way to a man who would soon no longer want to have anything to do with her——

'Don't you know that you're beautiful, Matty?' he said, his voice, his face, deadly and intent. 'But that's not why I want to marry you either. I want to marry you because I love you. It started a long time ago, you know. There was something in you that I loved when first I met you. I was cynically sure then that you were going to be totally corrupted by modern casual morals —by living with people who didn't care what you did. I was angry about the whole set-up, and I said things to hurt you, to frighten you. And they did, didn't they?' He paused and she nodded imperceptibly.

'When we met again,' he continued, 'I discovered by degrees that you hadn't been demoralised. But even before I was sure of that I knew you were the one woman I wanted to marry. If I hadn't been told by Jerry Bridle —and thank God I was, all things considered—that you were on the look-out for a husband, I'd have done things quite differently. As it was, I had to get in first, before someone else nabbed you.' The corners of his mouth tilted in a faint smile. 'I guess I didn't put on a very admirable show one way or another, but I thought you were learning to love and to trust me.'

'But——' Matty began, and stopped. She didn't altogether understand and she couldn't altogether believe, much as she wanted to. To tell him now, I haven't a penny—what would that do? It would bring another sort of truth out into the open, of course—and it had to be done.

But before she could say it, Dirk reached forward and took one of her hands in his. 'Matty,' he said, 'I've got to say this to you, but for God's sake don't think I'm maligning your uncle. I don't know exactly who put this idea into your head that my motive for marrying you was money, but believe me it's quite wrong. Moonak doesn't need money—everything's fine on my cattle station. But even if I wanted money—well, I'm afraid you're going to discover you're not an heiress after all, darling. I don't know what's left of the investments your mother left you, but I suspect it may be very little. I suspect, in fact, that that's one reason why Jerry Bridle's so keen to see you provided for. Whatever you believe, he's a gambler, and your mother was mistaken if she thought he was reformed. I'm not the only one to wonder how he ever managed to invest in expensive racehorses, you know.'

Matty was staring at him, her eyes wide and incredulous, her heart beating madly. So he knew—he'd guessed. So he wasn't marrying her for her money. So he did—he did love her——

With a little choked cry, she put her cheek down on his hand and tasted the salt of her tears. He knew—and he loved her. It was like a miracle.

She didn't resist now when he drew her into his arms.

'Don't cry about it, darling. I won't let you starve to death—I'll look after you. I'm sorry I had to tell you, but you'd have to find out soon.'

Matty pressed her tear-stained face to his breast, feeling the warmth of his bare skin against her cheek, the roughness of his hair.

'I'm not crying about that, Dirk. It's—it's true about the money, but Jerry told me—before you invited me to Moonak. That was why I agreed to marry you—so he wouldn't worry ... I'm crying because you love me,' she finished on a little laugh.

'And you?' he said demandingly. 'Are you going to admit——'

'That I love you—that I can't live without you,' she breathed. He tilted her face to his and she felt the pounding of his heart as their lips clung together. Tonight she'd sleep alone in his bed, but soon—very soon —nothing would keep them apart, and she relaxed against him in silent promise that she was ready to be his without restraint.